FALLING FOR IRISH
MACARTHUR FAMILY SERIES

Katie Reus

Copyright © 2021 by Katie Reus.

All rights reserved. Except as permitted under the U.S. Copyright Act of 1976, no part of this publication may be reproduced, distributed, or transmitted in any form or by any means, or stored in a database or retrieval system, without the prior written permission of the author. Thank you for buying an authorized version of this book and complying with copyright laws. You're supporting writers and encouraging creativity.

Cover art: Jaycee of Sweet 'N Spicy Designs
Editor: Julia Ganis
Author website: https://www.katiereus.com

Publisher's Note: This is a work of fiction. Names, characters, places, and incidents are either the products of the author's imagination or used fictitiously, and any resemblance to actual persons, living or dead, or business establishments, organizations or locales is completely coincidental.

Falling for Irish/Katie Reus. -- 1st ed.
KR Press, LLC

ISBN 13: 9781635561524

eISBN: 9781635561517

For my sister.

Praise for the novels of Katie Reus

"...a wild hot ride for readers. The story grabs you and doesn't let go."
—*New York Times* bestselling author, Cynthia Eden

"Has all the right ingredients: a hot couple, evil villains, and a killer action-filled plot.... [The] Moon Shifter series is what I call Grade-A entertainment!" —Joyfully Reviewed

"I could not put this book down.... Let me be clear that I am not saying that this was a good book *for* a paranormal genre; it was an excellent romance read, *period*." —All About Romance

"Reus strikes just the right balance of steamy sexual tension and nail-biting action....This romantic thriller reliably hits every note that fans of the genre will expect." —*Publishers Weekly*

"Prepare yourself for the start of a great new series! . . . I'm excited about reading more about this great group of characters."
—Fresh Fiction

"Wow! This powerful, passionate hero sizzles with sheer deliciousness. I loved every sexy twist of this fun & exhilarating tale. Katie Reus delivers!" —Carolyn Crane, RITA award winning author

"A sexy, well-crafted paranormal romance that succeeds with smart characters and creative world building." —Kirkus Reviews

"*Mating Instinct*'s romance is taut and passionate . . . Katie Reus's newest installment in her Moon Shifter series will leave readers breathless!"
—Stephanie Tyler, *New York Times* bestselling author

"You'll fall in love with Katie's heroes."
—*New York Times* bestselling author, Kaylea Cross

"Both romantic and suspenseful, a fast-paced sexy book full of high stakes action." —Heroes and Heartbreakers

"Katie Reus pulls the reader into a story line of second chances, betrayal, and the truth about forgotten lives and hidden pasts."
—The Reading Café

"Nonstop action, a solid plot, good pacing, and riveting suspense."
—RT Book Reviews

"Exciting in more ways than one, well-paced and smoothly written, I'd recommend *A Covert Affair* to any romantic suspense reader."
—Harlequin Junkie

"Sexy military romantic suspense." —USA Today

"Enough sexual tension to set the pages on fire."
—*New York Times* bestselling author, Alexandra Ivy

"*Avenger's Heat* hits the ground running...This is a story of strength, of partnership and healing, and it does it brilliantly."
—Vampire Book Club

"*Mating Instinct* was a great read with complex characters, serious political issues and a world I am looking forward to coming back to."
—All Things Urban Fantasy

CHAPTER ONE

Kathryn Irish's heels clicked across the lobby floor of the Davis Building as she headed for the bank of elevators. She felt weird being in her ex-boyfriend's building but the chances of running into Daniel MacArthur here were very small.

Daniel's company had hired Tony Domínguez, head of the East Coast division for Security Solutions and Analytics, Inc., to do a diagnostics check of their new security system and protocols. And Tony had hired her, since she was one of his preferred contractors. She wasn't exclusive to him—wasn't exclusive to anyone, and she liked it that way. It was just dumb luck that this was one of Daniel's buildings.

Under normal circumstances she wouldn't have taken a job at her ex's place, but the money was too good to pass up. He didn't work out of this building even if he did own it.

So here she was, posing as an engaged woman to talk to Helen Marr, owner of White Sands Event Planning. She just needed to get to the eighth floor so she could work her magical hacking skills. She'd done an analysis of the new security and the building itself, and had deemed this the easiest way to infiltrate and pinpoint any security holes.

As she waited in line at the bank of six elevators, she swore she could feel eyes on her. A little tingle started at the back of her neck and she automatically reached up to rub it. She looked at the others waiting for the elevators, wondering what was wrong with her.

Then she glanced over her shoulder and froze for all of a second before turning back around. *Oh, God!*

"Kathryn." That deep voice was nearly too much for her to handle.

She inwardly winced as the big, imposing man slid up next to her. His familiar masculine scent teased her nose. It was a woodsy, citrusy scent that made her think of Daniel and sex. She went weak in the knees, just like that. She couldn't believe he was here, but she pasted on a smile and turned to look up at sexy Daniel MacArthur. Since he was six foot four, she always had to look up, even though she was wearing heels today. For a moment all she could see were his pale blue eyes, staring down at her with an intensity she felt to her core. "Daniel," she rasped out, then cleared her throat. "I, ah, didn't think you came into this office very often." And never on Fridays. She knew that from simple recon. On Fridays he always, *always* worked out of the building on Prescott Street—well, apparently not. And planning the job today had hinged on him being gone.

He watched her with an unnerving intensity. "I had some stuff to take care of today. What are you even doing here..." His words trailed off as he glanced down at what she was holding.

Yikes, her stack of bridal magazines. And oh yeah, she was also sporting a huge engagement ring on her left ring finger. It was real too, though it wasn't hers.

He blinked once when he saw the ring, his expression darkening. Damn, the man was good-looking. It was no wonder he'd been voted one of the top twenty-five sexiest bachelors in the city the last five years in a row. His dark hair was a little longer than the normal close-cropped cut he'd kept when they'd been together. And she didn't think he'd shaved in a couple days, given the stubble he was sporting. Instead of looking unkempt, however, he simply looked even more delicious. Especially with some of his tattoos peeking out at his wrists. The man was always so buttoned up and professional looking, but underneath that suit? He had a surprising amount of ink and she loved every inch of it.

She hoped he wouldn't comment on the ring. Maybe he would just let her by without one single word about it. Maybe unicorns were real too. "I've got a meeting here on the eighth floor." She took a small step away from him, finding it easier to breathe with the little bit of distance between them.

He closed the distance in one step, not letting her move even an inch. "You're getting married?" he demanded as the elevators dinged.

Okay, so he wasn't letting this go. She was aware of people heading into the elevators, clearing out the whole area, but all she could focus on was him. It was like he was a magnet, pulling her in. She wanted to run away from him, to simply jump into the cluster of people and avoid this whole conversation. But she also didn't want him to realize that she was here on a job. She needed to be polite for another minute or two before making her escape. "It would appear so." That wasn't a lie, exactly. And she hated lying to him. Even if he had broken her heart.

"But…" He cleared his throat. "We've only been broken up for two months."

He seemed absolutely shocked that she'd moved on so fast, which was a little ironic considering she'd seen a picture of him with some svelte blonde wrapped around him on a trashy blog the other day. Okay that was a lie—there had been no wrapping around him, but they had been standing next to each other and smiling pleasantly at the camera. Still, the memory of that picture and the stupid byline that had gone with it rankled Kathryn. *Sexy Bachelor and Heiress Caught Canoodling!* Ugh. Just remembering that eased her guilt. And what kind of publication used the word canoodling? Even a trashy one? Seriously.

She absolutely wasn't commenting on that. "Look, I don't want to be late for my appointment."

For the first time since she'd known him, he looked completely out of sorts, his pale eyes searching hers for something. When there was a shout from across the lobby, Daniel turned in that direction, his expression growing dark.

She knew exactly what was going on because this was part of the plan with her partner.

"What the hell!" someone shouted. "Stop that!"

She suppressed a smile when she saw a whole bunch of balloons being released. And then…bubbles came out of nowhere, being pumped throughout the lobby. Bubbles were something new and it made her giggle, despite this whole situation. "Looks like you've got your hands full," she said, moving toward an elevator that opened.

"Wait," he started, then turned back at another annoyed shout from security.

Seeing her opportunity, she slid into the elevator and quickly pressed the close door button while he was distracted. The last thing she saw was his annoyingly sexy, brooding face as he stared at her while the doors swished shut on him.

As soon as they did, she slumped against the back wall and closed her eyes for a long moment as the elevator ascended. Her stomach rolled once and it had nothing to do with the ride.

For a moment she wondered if he would figure out why she was really here today. He knew some of what she did for her contract work, but she'd never shared the details of how she worked jobs—it was confidential and she wouldn't have given away her trade secrets regardless. Getting her bonus depended on not being discovered during the actual infiltration.

She doubted he would suspect her of being here for anything other than what it appeared she was here for. She was just second-guessing herself and she needed to keep it together.

As she stepped out of the elevator and into the waiting area of White Sands Event Planning, a pretty woman with dark, corkscrew curls smiled at her from behind the reception desk. "Hello, how may I help you today?"

"Hi, I'm Kathryn and I have a meeting with Helen."

"Of course. My name is Sonya," she said, standing and smoothing down her gray pencil skirt. "Can I get you a latte, sparkling water, something to eat?"

"A latte would be great," she said as she followed Sonya down the hallway. The walls were a soft gray, with black-and-white photos from various events—mainly weddings—hanging every couple feet. All happy, smiling people. There were also a few images of clearly custom-made cakes and a couple brides in couture dresses.

Sonya showed Kathryn to a conference room that was feminine and comfortable. It was also filled with art showcasing the company's events—more happy people. This was nothing like the boring boardrooms she'd been in so many times before as part of her job.

"Make yourself comfortable. Helen is running a little bit behind, but she'll be with you within the next ten minutes. And I'll be back with your drink. Oh, we've also got petit fours and scones if you're interested. They're all from the bakery we use for weddings."

Under normal circumstances Kathryn would've said yes to all of the food, but not right now. Her stomach was knotted too tight. "I'm going to pass on the food, but would you mind telling me where your restrooms are?"

"Of course." She pointed down the hallway and gave brief directions before hurrying off in the other direction in five-inch stilettos.

Kathryn left most of her stuff on the table but slipped out her slim laptop and tucked it in the back of her skirt, then adjusted her jacket over it. She ducked out of the conference room and hurried down the hallway, her heart racing.

She'd completed almost fifty infiltrations over the last few years and had been successful with every single one of them. But it felt weird to be hacking into Daniel MacArthur's system. It was what he'd paid her boss for, but still, knowing he was in the building right now while she worked was strange. It also made her really, *really* not want to get caught. When he'd hired Tony to do this random check of security, Tony had only given him a vague week's time frame for when he should expect the hack to occur. It wouldn't do them much good if they knew exactly when to look for a hack because they would have tightened security.

The restroom was empty so she hurried into one of the stalls and unlocked the door. Then she sat on the toilet lid and got to work, her keyboard whisper quiet. A minute later when she heard someone step inside, she paused for only a moment before getting back to work. When she heard water running and then the hand dryer, she breathed a sigh of relief as she slid her way into the building's security system.

The way his system had been created, anyone who wanted access had to be in the building to infiltrate it. And right now she was hacking into a Wi-Fi modem that hadn't been updated within the last couple days. It was how she would eventually work her way into the rest of the system. She wouldn't be able to get into his financials or anything, but she would be able to screw with his security system, which was a huge deal if someone wanted to do a specific type of job against his place.

Once she'd maneuvered through a back door and left a little message for the security team, she tucked her laptop back in her skirt and hurried out, washing her hands and drying them before booking it back to the conference room. She was just getting settled and taking a sip of her now almost cold latte when a woman with a whole lot of blonde hair and a big smile hurried into the room.

"I'm Helen, and I'm so sorry I'm late," she said.

It was hard not to smile at the woman. "Don't worry about it. I'm just relaxing in this wonderful conference room. I love the way you've set everything up." Instead of all stiff-backed chairs, there were a couple individual seating areas filled with cushy chairs in shades of purple and gray.

"Thank you. Are you hungry? Need a refill?" Helen asked as she shook Kathryn's hand and sat across from her in a matching tufted purple chair.

"No, I'm fine, but thank you."

The woman's phone buzzed a few times but she ignored it.

"Do you need to get that?"

"Normally I would say no—normally I wouldn't even have it on me, but I might need to grab this. There's been some type of breach downstairs and security is going crazy. I think they might end up doing a walk-through of each of our floors, since we rent from the MacArthur Company and their security oversees the whole building."

"Did you want to reschedule? If it would make it easier for you?" Kathryn really hoped so, because then she wouldn't have to go through a whole charade and lie to the woman. Even though this was a free consultation, Kathryn's employer would end up sending a check to Helen for wasting her time. It was the only thing that eased her guilt at taking up Helen's time under false pretenses.

"Oh, no, I don't want to do that." But Kathryn could see that the woman did want to do just that.

So she stood and smiled. "Look, I've heard great things about your company. Let's just reschedule for later in the week, okay? That way no one's rushed or stressed out."

Relief spread across the woman's face as she stood. "I think that might be better. And I will make sure my assistant reschedules you immediately."

Kathryn squashed another bit of guilt she experienced because she wouldn't be rescheduling at all, but that was just part of this job.

It didn't take long to make it down to the lobby. Kathryn couldn't fight the nerves humming through her as she descended in the elevator. Once she stepped out into the lobby, she spotted Daniel talking to two security guys forty feet away. Good, he was occupied.

The main exit had a bunch of men and women standing there, talking to her partner, Quincy. She was too far away to hear how the conversation was going, but he'd done this enough times that she knew exactly how Quincy was playing this thing off. Right now he'd be claiming that everything had just been a prank. Usually he could convince people he was harmless—he had that whole charming boyish thing about him.

She wasn't sure if it would work on Daniel's people, but as long as she got out of the building, that was all that mattered. Because they couldn't arrest Quincy for anything. He might get fined, but then of course it would get thrown out once Daniel realized they were the ones he had actually hired to scan the security here.

Moving quickly, she cursed her loud heels as she hurried toward the front door. Pulling out her phone, she stopped herself from looking in Daniel's direction even though she didn't actually pull up anything on her screen. Sooooo close. She was almost to the exit.

"Ma'am? *Ma'am?*"

Jolted out of her internal getaway pep talk, she turned to find a man in a security uniform striding toward her. "Yes?" she asked.

"We're checking the bags of everyone who leaves. I'm going to need you to come with me over to the tables we've got set up." He motioned to where they had indeed set up a handful of tables off to one side and were now checking everyone's bags like at an airport.

She stared at him, acting confused. "What? Why?"

"Henry, it's fine," Daniel said, hurrying over toward them. His gaze flicked down to her left hand, his expression darkening for an instant before he looked back at Henry again. "She's fine."

"But Mr. MacArthur, protocol says—"

"I know what the protocol says. She's fine."

The man nodded once and backed away.

Daniel looked her up and down, a quick sweep that was anything but clinical. "You're leaving so soon?"

She ignored that heated look, unsure what to even make of it. "Yeah, I guess something is going on with security?" She pointed over at the tables. "We decided to reschedule."

He nodded and kept watching her.

She shifted on her feet. Had he changed his mind about searching her stuff? "Ah, your guy can look in my purse if he wants." She held her big purse out and started to open it, but he just waved a hand at it.

"You look really good," he said quietly, his voice as intense as his gaze.

Oh. Wow. For a moment she wanted to melt under that gaze. "So do you," she said just as quietly, unable to get anything more out. And it was true. He somehow looked even better than she remembered, which just seemed unfair. She'd tried to convince herself that she'd worked him up in her mind, that of course he wasn't as sexy as she'd remembered. All lies.

"I've missed you," he blurted out, surprising her, and she was pretty sure he'd surprised himself with the admission if his expression was anything to go on.

She stared at him in shock, mainly because this was something she'd never expected from him. It was so raw and real, and for this one moment, Daniel wasn't wearing a mask. He wasn't the mysterious and closed-off man she'd shared a whole lot of orgasms with.

Oh God. She didn't know how to deal with this. "Oh, ah… I…" She didn't want to tell him she missed him too because it would give him an opening. And it would just rip her heart open all over again. Even if it was the truth.

"Mr. MacArthur." A woman wearing heels and a sharp business suit hurried over to them, nodding at Kathryn once. Then she murmured something to Daniel, so Kathryn took the opportunity to slip away. She headed straight for the security guard named Henry, who only nodded politely at her and motioned that she was okay to leave without a bag check.

She heard Daniel curse behind her but she ignored him and resisted the urge to sprint the last few feet out the door. She wanted out and it had nothing to do with the job. Nope, she just needed to get away from Daniel and his ice-blue eyes.

Daniel with the wicked grin and talented hands that had turned her to mush once upon a time.

Once she was outside in the bright sunshine, she slid her sunglasses on and sucked in a sharp breath. She felt as if the weight of the entire building had been lifted off her shoulders as she hurried to the waiting car.

They'd pulled it off.

But for reasons she understood very well, she didn't have that normal high she got after completing a job. No, she just felt…hollow and wrung out.

CHAPTER TWO

Daniel wanted to run after Kathryn, but what the hell was he going to do? Beg her to talk to him? Demand that she take off that stupid ring so he could throw it in an incinerator? The ring that was *very* definitely real. He recognized quality when he saw it.

Not that he was surprised someone had scooped her up. She was a diamond in the rough and he'd been stupid enough to let her walk away. Unfortunately he still wasn't sure what he'd done wrong. One moment they'd been on their way to a date and then she was suddenly telling him that it was over, that she'd realized she wasn't interested in a serious relationship. That what they'd had was finished.

To say he'd been blindsided was an understatement. He still hadn't recovered—or figured out what had gone wrong. Maybe all the overtime he'd been working back then? After she'd ended things he'd tried to talk to her about it—multiple times—but she'd blown him off. Seeing her today had him rattled.

She'd looked good too. No, she'd looked *stunning*. He was used to seeing her in jeans and T-shirts but today she'd been wearing a dress that showed off all her curves—and legs he was obsessed with. She wasn't tall, just average in height, but she did a lot of yoga and swimming and her legs... He had to actively stop thinking about the many times she'd had the sexiest legs ever thrown over his shoulders as he went down on her. Brought her pleasure. Gave her orgasms. Damn it—he had to stop obsessing but it was hard when she'd been here in the flesh.

He'd had to resist the urge to run his hands through her long, auburn hair, to touch what most definitely wasn't his anymore.

He was determined to finally get answers. She might be wearing a ring, but he couldn't kill that small kernel of hope inside him that maybe he still had a chance.

He walked away from his assistant, waving her off as she tried to keep talking to him, and pulled out his cell phone.

"Hey, now's not a good time," his sister Sienna whispered.

"Why not? What are you doing?"

"I'm on a job," she whispered again. "But you never call, so I answered. Is everything okay? Is it Mom and Dad?"

He ignored her questions. "Why the hell didn't you tell me that Kathryn is engaged?"

There was a moment of silence. "Kathryn's not engaged. I would know, trust me."

Hope shot through him, painful and intense. Just as quickly, he squashed it. "When was the last time you saw her?" Because that ring had been very real. And she'd been carrying bridal magazines, on her way to meet a wedding planner. Kathryn! The woman who'd once told him she thought most weddings were ostentatious, and that if she ever got married, she'd just elope.

"I've been really busy this month. I don't know... Hell, I guess it's been almost two months since you guys broke up and I haven't seen her since... Oh, shit, I'm a totally crap friend," she muttered to herself. "I've talked to her and we've texted but I haven't seen her in two months."

"I just saw her and she had a giant rock on her finger." His fingers tightened around his phone. And she'd been practically glowing, her green eyes bright and captivating.

"Well, what do you want me to do about it? Break the guy's kneecaps?" She snorted.

"Call her and find out about him."

"Are you hiring me? Because I'm not going to stalk a friend."

His sister was a PI, and even though he'd offered her a job at his company many times over, she always turned him down, preferring to make her own way instead. Something he respected.

"No, don't spy on her. I mean, maybe spy a little bit." He scrubbed a hand over his face.

"Oh my God, I'm not having this conversation and I'm not spying on my friend. I've gotta go." The line went dead.

Daniel cursed and nearly crushed his phone, but since he didn't want to have to go through the hassle of replacing it, he simply shoved it into his pocket. He had to deal with this mess here and then he would figure out what to do about Kathryn.

He'd thought he could move on, could somehow live without her. She'd made it clear she wanted nothing to do with him. But after seeing her today? The attraction burned even brighter between them and he'd seen the look in her eyes. She might be engaged to another man, but she still wanted him.

That changed everything.

If she still wanted him, he wasn't letting her go without a fight.

* * *

Three hours later, Kathryn slid into the booth across from Quincy. "How long did they keep you?"

He grinned and waved at their server before holding up two fingers. For two drinks, she assumed.

"I hope you ordered something for me too," she said, laughing.

"Yeah, I told him what to bring when a pretty redhead got here. And to answer your first question, they just let me go half an hour ago."

She raised her eyebrows. "Dang."

"Technically I could have left at any time but I played nice since they never called the cops—and I just acted stupid. Their security had a bunch of questions and I'm pretty sure someone on their security team tried to follow me, but I lost them." His grin widened, revealing a dimple.

She snickered. "What was up with the bubbles?" He hadn't told her about that part of the distraction.

"I decided to mix things up a bit. Oh, and I saw you talking to Daniel Mac-Hottie-Arthur. I thought we were screwed when I saw that but then he let you go. What did the big man want anyway?"

She'd worked with Quincy on and off for two years. For the most part she kept her work and personal life separate—though she and Quincy had always been open about their personal lives. Until she'd started dating Daniel. She adored Quincy but Daniel had been this huge force of nature and she'd kept Daniel's name private for the three months they'd been together. Well, with the exception of her closest friends, because she had confided in her book club about him. But that was different. "Ah, well, remember that whirlwind relationship I had that ended two months ago?"

He blinked once and then his eyes widened. "Are you kidding me? You and MacArthur?"

"Yep."

"Wait, doesn't he know what you do for a living?"

"Sort of. If he guessed at why I was there, he didn't let on. And honestly, when he saw my engagement ring, I think it threw him off more than anything. He might realize the truth later. Either way, we did a good job."

"That we did." He took the beer the server dropped off and clinked the top against Kathryn's.

"We kicked ass," she added, feeling a little smug. Infiltrating his system had taken a certain amount of finesse.

"So why didn't you tell me about him before?" Quincy asked before taking another sip of his beer.

"I wasn't sure where the relationship was going." And it turned out the answer was nowhere so she was glad she'd kept it to herself.

At the time she'd liked having him all to herself—though her brothers had known because they were nosy and knew everything. But she and Daniel had managed to keep all mentions of their relationship out of any sort of society rag. He hadn't cared about the gossip stuff, but she'd wanted to be damn sure they had a future before she was publicly linked to him. She hadn't wanted any sort of media scrutiny.

Sure, it would have been on a local level, but that was too much for something that wasn't serious. Now she was glad she'd listened to her instinct and insisted on keeping things quiet. The breakup had been one of the hardest things she'd ever dealt with. If she'd had to do it while being watched by the media, it would have been a hundred times harder. "But it's all fine between us. He was perfectly polite when we ran into each other." He'd also been looking at her with that familiar hunger. Which just made the ache in her chest even worse.

Quincy snickered at that. "There's got to be some cosmic justice in that, you getting a fat bonus from this job."

She didn't bother hiding her smile. "Maybe so."

"So…you're not going to give me any juicy details? Like why y'all broke up?"

"Not unless you tell me why you and Mr. Bartender broke up last week." Unlike Kathryn, Quincy told her every single detail of his dating life. And she knew this would be the perfect distraction.

"Oh, I'll tell you. I thought he was pretty cool so I invited him to a house party—where he proceeded to pull his dick out."

She blinked. "What? I'm going to need way more details than this."

Quincy took a sip of his beer then set it down. By his expression, she knew she was in for a good story. "A bunch of us started playing poker. Then someone of course suggested strip poker. So Mr. Bartender pulls off his pants, then his boxers when he loses a couple rounds. I mean, who does that? You start with your shoes or shirt."

She snickered at the image. "So he was just sitting around with a shirt on and his dick hanging out?"

"Yep. My friends thought it was hilarious but I was a little horrified. I mean, I still slept with him, but—"

A laugh burst out of her. "Seriously?"

He shrugged, his grin widening. "I'd already seen a nice preview of what to expect."

"Impressive?"

"Oh yeah."

"But you still ended things with him?"

"Yep. He tried to get me to do CrossFit with him. I do not need that in my life."

She laughed even harder. "You're ridiculous!"

Quincy shrugged, but still grinned.

"Your dating stories are always so much better than mine."

"This is true," he said, waving off their server and declining another drink since his was still half full.

"My last date was kind of a nightmare too."

"Ooooh, are you getting personal with me?" He raised his eyebrows.

She shrugged. "There's not that much to tell. He was just a jackass. He talked the whole time, and when he would ask me a question I would start to answer it, but he'd cut me off before I could finish. Like every single time. It was all I could do not to run out of there."

Quincy shook his head. "You can't even give me a teeny bit of details about you and MacArthur? That man is seriously fine."

"No," she said quietly, and the pain must have shown on her face because his eyes widened slightly.

"Shit, I'm sorry. I didn't know you were really into him. Damn, so does that mean I need to make a voodoo doll of him tonight and set it on fire?"

She lifted a shoulder. "Maybe... No, he wasn't that bad." He'd just thought she was after him for his money.

"Well I'm guessing he wasn't that good either, if you're sitting across from me looking all sad. I'm kind of surprised you didn't destroy his life with your hacking skills."

"Hey! I only use my skills for good." Mostly anyway.

He simply lifted an eyebrow. "If in like a month or two I read about him losing millions of dollars in some freak banking error, it's not you?"

She laughed at Quincy's antics and shook her head. "I will not be getting any sort of revenge. Trust me. I just want him out of my life." It was the only way she'd get over her heartbreak. Because after two months, her heart still wasn't healed.

"Well, I'll be your alibi if you do get revenge."

She just snorted as their server returned to the table. They grabbed a couple appetizers and water. Half an hour later, she said goodbye and headed home. It was pretty late for her to be getting home anyway. Most of her jobs ended by five or six o'clock but no way would she have headed home after this one without seeing Quincy in person. She'd wanted to find out how things had gone once she'd left. And okay, she'd wanted to know if anything had happened with Daniel.

Kathryn pulled into her designated parking lot at her condominium. She loved living in the small complex, though in the last couple months she'd felt like she was missing something. Of course she knew exactly what that feeling was.

She missed Daniel.

But she had to stop thinking about him. On instinct, she pulled out her house keys and the attached pepper spray. Both her brothers were in law enforcement, and Carson—the oldest—had drilled taking protective measures into her head at a young age. He'd made it clear that she shouldn't have to protect herself—that he was pretty disappointed with the male gender in general—but that she still needed to. It wasn't like she needed him to push her; she lived in the real world.

She knew she had to be able to take care of herself.

Grabbing her purse and laptop as well, she slid out of the car and pressed the key fob to lock it. A cool January breeze rolled over her as she stepped up onto the sidewalk. The many palm trees lining the entire place rustled with the wind. Since summer was on the way—Florida just skipped spring and went straight to humid summer—she was enjoying the respite from the heat.

As she turned the corner of the building onto the connecting sidewalk, a shadow to her left caught her eye. Her breath caught in her throat as a big male figure peeled off the building.

Her instinct was to freeze up, but thanks to a whole lot of defense training from her brother, she let out a scream when she saw a masked man rushing toward her. She jerked her hand up and started spraying wildly at his covered face.

"Shit," the guy growled, clearly surprised. Then he started clawing at his eyes and screaming along with her.

Kathryn kept spraying until he fell to his knees.

As he hit the ground, she sprinted in the other direction, her shoes snapping loudly along the sidewalk. Her phone was somewhere in the depths of her giant purse and she didn't dare stop to try and find it.

Heart in her throat, she sprinted as fast as she could until she made it to the stairs to her building. She risked a glance over her shoulder as she raced up the stairs. No one was chasing after her. As she reached the top, she let out a scream as two big hands steadied her upper arms...

Wait, Daniel? She stared up at him, eyes wide.

He continued to hold on to her, his expression concerned. "Kathryn? What's wrong?"

"A man in a mask jumped out at me. I pepper-sprayed him," she managed to rasp out even though she was breathing erratically and couldn't stop trembling. She couldn't believe something like this had happened again—after being mugged a couple weeks ago, this felt like life was just taking a crap on her.

Moving into action, he grabbed her keys from her hands. "Inside, now."

She was grateful he was steady because she didn't trust herself to even open the front door because of how badly her fingers were shaking. How was that for a good getaway? She couldn't even get herself to safety she was trembling so bad.

He shut and locked the door behind them even as he held his cell phone up to his ear. "Yes, this is an emergency. My name is Daniel MacArthur and I'm at…" Daniel spoke quietly into his phone, clearly talking to emergency services.

He was calling the police, of course. Her reaction time was far too slow right now. She moved to the security pad and disarmed her security system as he continued talking, her fingers unsteady on the buttons.

Feeling almost numb, she walked into the kitchen and dropped her purse and keys onto the center island. Her place wasn't big so she could easily see him through the open bar area facing her living room, looking like emperor of the world in his expensive business suit as he spoke in clipped, efficient tones to the operator.

"I'll be waiting outside for the officer," he said before ending the call. Then he strode quickly into the kitchen.

Meanwhile she felt as if she was on autopilot, as if someone had pressed the pause button on her brain. What had just happened felt surreal, as if it had happened to someone else. And it had all gone down so fast. First she'd been thinking of the nice weather and then a monster had jumped out at her from the shadows.

Scanning her from head to toe in a clinical fashion, he frowned. "Did anything else happen?"

She shook her head, wrapping her arms around herself even as her cat, Mr. Twinkles, appeared out of nowhere, meowing up at them. "No. I...it all happened so fast. He jumped out at me like a ninja and I just reacted and started spraying. And screaming."

His frown didn't let up even as he glanced down at Mr. Twinkles. "Smart thinking, pepper-spraying him."

"I can thank my brother for that."

Daniel's mouth curved up slightly as he picked up her whining cat. "Your brothers do have some uses."

She snorted softly because he'd always butted heads with her brothers—probably because he'd been dating their little sister. Her gaze narrowed as Mr. Twinkles cuddled up to him, nuzzling his head against Daniel's chin. That little traitor!

"Did you want to call anyone? Your brother? Your...fiancé?" He practically spat out the last word even as he gently petted her cat's head.

Fiancé? It took a moment for her to realize what he meant. She looked away from him and shook her head.

She still needed to return the ring to her boss and couldn't believe she'd forgotten to this afternoon. "I'll call my brother later and let him know what's going on. But not now. He's already off work and I don't want him to call up our parents and worry them." Her parents were divorced but the one thing they could agree on was that they loved their kids. And her mom would be over here in minutes, quickly followed by her father. Then it would somehow devolve into them arguing and she simply couldn't deal with that now.

Daniel nodded, still watching her closely. "It'll take the cops a few minutes to get here if you want to change into something more comfortable," he said quietly. "Or I can pour you a glass of wine?" The concern rolling off him was palpable and it shook her to her core.

Why was he even here? She wanted to ask him, but decided to wait until after she'd dealt with the cops. One problem at a time. She rubbed a hand over her face and shook her head. "No, but thank you. I'll need to make a statement and I don't want any alcohol on my breath for that. Hopefully they won't make me go down to the station for something like this. Or I don't think they will."

"Okay, then I'll head outside and wait." He gently put down a now annoyed Mr. Twinkles before he strode out the front door, looking like a warrior going into battle.

She could admit that she felt better with him being there. He'd reacted to everything so quickly and efficiently, just taking charge. Sometimes it had annoyed her when he'd just taken over when they'd been together, but in times like this, in any sort of crisis, he was definitely the man you wanted on your side. He never seemed to lose his head.

Though she didn't feel like drinking, she did decide to change out of her dress, so she hurried to her room and slipped into a comfortable pair of lounge pants and a pullover sweater. It had actually been a gift from Daniel, and she thought about taking it off when she realized that, but screw it. He'd given it to her and it was one of her favorites. Right now it made her feel better. Once she was dressed, she opened up a can of food for Mr. Twinkles—who forgot everything else existed when food was concerned—and left him to it.

As she stepped into the living room, Daniel was coming in from the front door as well, a detective with him.

One she recognized. Despite the situation, she smiled at the other man. "Mendoza, apparently I keep running into you."

The fit, very attractive Latino detective smiled at her. "Hey, Irish. I like seeing you, but I wish it was under better circumstances. I didn't call Carson about this since he's already off work. Should I call him for moral support?"

She shook her head. "No. You know he can't get involved in a case that involves me anyway. And really, I'm just making a report. I didn't even see the guy's face, and if you tell Carson..."

Mendoza snorted. "The whole Irish clan will descend on you."

Exactly. "Did you want coffee or anything?" It was late, but she also knew he would be working a later shift since he was here.

He shook his head and then motioned for her and Daniel to sit. "I'm good. Why don't you run through everything with me from the beginning?"

Daniel sat directly next to her, not holding her hand, but she felt his steady presence nonetheless as his knee pressed up against hers. As she relayed what happened, that band around her chest got even tighter.

It didn't take long for her to give her statement, while Mendoza silently took notes and only interrupted with minimal questions. Once he was finished, he looked between the two of them before focusing on her. "Look, I don't like that something has happened to you twice in the last couple weeks. I mean, this is a big city and shit happens, but is there anything going on at work? Any bad dates? Anything you can think of that could be the driving force behind this? Other than a coincidence?"

"What happened in the last couple weeks?" Daniel interjected, watching her.

"Ah, I was mugged a couple weeks ago leaving a job. It's nothing. The guy snatched my bag and got my keys and wallet. I had to cancel my credit cards and—"

"Did you change your locks?" he growled out.

"Yes. Carson changed my locks that night. And I changed my security code for good measure. Luckily my phone was on me and not in my purse."

The tension in his shoulders eased a little bit, but not by much.

"All right, Kathryn," Mendoza said as he stood. "I'll be in touch if we find anything out. I'll talk to the property management company and see if I can get a look at their security feeds. I saw a couple cameras on the way in here. They're closed now, but I'll talk to them in the morning. Just make sure you lock your doors and pay attention to your surroundings. You saved yourself a whole lot of grief by thinking so quickly and pepper-spraying him." His tone shifted slightly as he continued. "I'm just glad this story didn't have a different ending."

Yeah, she was too. She suppressed another shudder as she thought of what could have happened if the man had gotten her.

She walked Mendoza to the door, and after he left she shut and locked it. Now it was time to deal with Daniel. "Not that I don't appreciate it," she said as she turned to find Daniel standing next to her couch. He looked so huge and imposing next to the leather sofa she normally curled up on with her e-reader or paperback at night. "But what are you doing here?"

"I just wanted to see you. Today felt kind of strange between us. I...should have called," he said on a wince.

"Well, yeah, you should have." She laughed a little awkwardly. "But I'm sorry I ran out of there before. It just looked like you had a lot to deal with." Mostly the truth. She wasn't sorry she'd run. Even if she hadn't been on a job, she would have run.

He watched her closely with those pale blue eyes she'd found captivating right from the start. "Are you sure you don't want to call your fiancé?"

Ugh. She couldn't deal with this right now. "I don't want to talk about that."

"Well if you were mine, I would want to know if—"

"Well I'm not yours. And when we were together you thought I was after your money," she snapped without meaning to. The events of the night piled onto her and the pulsing headache that had started minutes ago was spreading along the back of her skull as she stepped toward him. "And I seriously can't deal with this tonight. You need to leave now."

She didn't give a crap why he'd stopped by at this point. She needed a hot shower and sleep. And she really needed to call her brother, because she didn't want him to hear about this from Detective Mendoza. She'd just make Carson promise not to call their parents before she told him what was going on.

Daniel stared at her, a scowl on his face. "What the hell are you talking about? After my money?"

She snorted in derision as she strode past him and unlocked her door. Then she gestured toward it. "I am asking you to leave now. Don't make me ask the detective to come back up here and escort you out."

His expression went thunderous at her words but he did as she said and stepped outside. "Kathryn—"

"Nope. If you want to talk, next time call me." Feeling a bit mean, she shut the door in his face and quickly locked it.

"Kathryn," he called out.

"Go away," she muttered, too low for him to hear.

"Set your security system."

Even though she rolled her eyes at his tone, she really appreciated the thoughtfulness. He'd always been like that, conscious of her security and wanting her to make sure she took care of herself and stayed safe. It was really hard to get mad at that even though she was frustrated with the sexy male in general. Why the hell had he just shown up tonight? He didn't have the right to do that anymore.

"I'm setting it now," she called out because she knew he wouldn't leave until she did exactly that.

After she did, she collapsed against the wall and rubbed a hand over her face. Was it a full moon out? Or maybe Mercury was in retrograde?

Whatever was going on, that ache in her head was nothing compared to the one in her chest. Seeing Daniel in person, especially back in her home, a place they'd gotten naked in many times, made her wish things could have been different.

But she knew they never could be. And it was something she would have to live with. When she opened her eyes, her traitorous little cat was looking up at her with judging eyes.

"Don't you start on me," she muttered.

Mr. Twinkles simply meowed before turning and giving her his swishing tail as he sauntered off to who knew where.

CHAPTER THREE

Five months ago

Kathryn pressed the elevator button at the Wilson Building downtown. As she waited, a tall man who smelled really, really good slid up next to her. Without looking at him, she inhaled the citrusy, woodsy scent. Damn, whatever that was, she could get high off it. You know, if she did that sort of thing. As if drawn by a magnet she glanced over—and found herself looking up. For a moment she froze as her gaze clashed with icy blue eyes.

The man looking at her smiled politely then sort of froze as he stared at her in turn. Good Lord, this man was *sexy*. She blinked once, feeling mesmerized, and tried to force a polite smile but...she just kept staring like a lunatic. When he kept looking at her too, she wondered if she had something on her face.

Even though she had the insane urge to check her teeth, she resisted and somehow tore her gaze away to stare at the elevator doors. As they stood there, she could feel his gaze on her.

Or maybe that was just wishful thinking.

When the elevator doors swooshed open, he motioned for her to enter. And as they stepped into the elevator together, whatever that subtle, sexy masculine scent was wrapped around her. She tried not to sniff like a weirdo as she pressed the button for the top floor. "Which floor?" she asked, too nervous to meet his gaze again.

"Same one," he said in a deep, delicious voice she felt all the way to her core.

Damn, that voice should be bottled up and sold. But only to *her*. Clearly she hadn't had sex in too long because she was starting to fantasize about some stranger in an elevator. And at that thought, she started thinking about elevator sex with this particular stranger. The man with pale blue eyes, dark hair and broad shoulders. Shoulders she could easily imagine holding on to as he pinned her up against this elevator wall.

Oh my God, stop it, she ordered herself. *Get it together!* After she'd caught her asshole ex cheating on her—freaking tale as old as time—she'd sworn off men for a while. But Tall, Dark and Mouthwateringly Hot was making her rethink that. As if drawn to him, she tried to sneak a peek at his face again and found him looking directly at her.

Their gazes clashed but he averted his almost immediately and looked forward again, his posture stiff.

As the elevator dinged, he made a motion for her to step out, depriving her of that sexy voice again. And a peek at his ass.

She felt self-conscious, especially since he was in a very expensive suit and she was wearing jeans, a green T-shirt that said *Hulk Mode On* and sparkly green sneakers. She wasn't sure why she was fantasizing about this guy when she had no doubt she wasn't his type. He probably went for tall, leggy women who dressed in pencil skirts, silk tops and five-inch heels.

When they both turned left into the hallway, she said, "I take it we're going to the same place." Then she inwardly cursed herself for her nervous chatter. Clearly they were going to the same place, *Captain Obvious*.

"Looks like it." He glanced at her, his gaze sweeping over her quickly before he glanced back ahead.

Finally, blessedly, they reached the end of the hallway. As they stepped into the only office at the end of it, her friend Chloe—who she was meeting to go book shopping with over her friend's lunch break—stood suddenly.

"Mr. MacArthur, you can go on back. He's expecting you." Then she nodded once at Kathryn before picking up the phone intercom. "I'm off to lunch but Mr. MacArthur is here for you. I'll see you in an hour." Her mouth curving into a smile, she grabbed her purse. "I'm ready to do some damage on my credit card."

Kathryn grinned. "Me too," she murmured before flicking a glance at the man whose name was apparently Mr. MacArthur.

He hadn't gone very far, and instead was watching her with a sexy sort of intensity she felt all the way to her core. *Oh wow*. Heat curled inside her from just one look from him. She wondered what he could do with more than that.

Somehow she tore her gaze away and joined Chloe. They were heading to a bookstore downtown owned by one of their friends—and then probably hitting up a shoe sale Chloe had been talking about. "So who was that?" Kathryn murmured as they reached the elevators. She didn't care that they were far out of earshot, she still didn't want to talk too loud in case he somehow overheard her.

"Who was who?"

"The man you called Mr. MacArthur. What's his story?"

Her friend shot her a sly look. "Why?"

"Because I have eyes and he was sexy as hell." Her cheeks flushed even as she said the words. It wasn't like he could overhear her, but still, they were in the same building and it felt weird.

Chloe's dark eyes widened slightly. "I thought you'd sworn off men."

She lifted a shoulder as they stepped into the elevator. Things changed.

"He's single as far as I know—not that I know much. He's always very polite, not the creep type if you know what I mean."

Of course she knew.

"I'll find out more about him if you want?"

She shook her head. "No way. It's not like I'm going to see him again. I was just being nosy because he was hot and it's been far too long since I've had sex." Besides, if she wanted to know more about him, she could find out on her own.

"Whose fault is that?" Flipping her dark hair over her shoulder, Chloe gave her a tart look as they stepped off the elevator.

"I feel like the answer you're looking for is mine."

"It *is* your fault. You get asked out all the time."

"Whatever. Let's go get some new books."

"And shoes."

"Definitely. I need some new sneakers too."

Chloe just snorted as she eyed Kathryn's sparkly ones—probably because she had like sixty pairs of sneakers—but then she grinned as they stepped out into the sunshine. "We need to get some kayak time this weekend."

Kathryn groaned slightly.

"What? The weather's gorgeous."

"You're always trying to make me get outside."

"Yeah, you need the vitamin D."

"Unlike you, I have to slather sunscreen on every inch of my body when we do." The curse of her redheaded coloring.

"We'll go early, then."

"All right." She actually didn't mind kayaking, but Chloe was way more outdoorsy than Kathryn. And she ran marathons.

That was something Kathryn would never understand—running for fun. The only time anyone would catch her running is if she was being chased by a rabid pack of dogs. She much preferred yoga and swimming.

By the time they'd made it back to Chloe's job, they were a few minutes late—so Kathryn gave her a quick hug before Chloe made a dash for the glass doors.

"This weekend, kayaking, don't forget," Chloe tossed over her shoulder before she hurried inside.

"You like kayaking?" The deep male voice made her turn around.

She recognized the voice instantly—she'd only heard it once but now it was etched into her brain. She found herself looking up into the handsome face of Mr. MacArthur. And she really wished she knew what his first name was now. "Ah, sort of."

"You sort of like kayaking?"

She glanced around, surprised this sexy god was talking to her. There was a car idling along the curb and she guessed it was waiting for him. A few people walked past them but the street was otherwise pretty quiet. Yep, he was talking to her. "Yeah, sort of. But I love my friend so I go with her. I mean, it's good exercise and she swears the vitamin D is good for me."

He chuckled slightly, giving her his full attention. Which was kind of unnerving. "What kinds of things do you like to do?"

Oh, she could think of a slew of things she'd like to do—to him. Wait, had she said that out loud? He wasn't looking at her weird so she must have kept it to herself. "Um, yoga, swimming, drinking too much chai and going on historic ghost tours." Oh God, this was like the worst dating profile description ever. What was wrong with her? Why couldn't she have given a normal answer? Yep, he was going to walk away now.

His mouth quirked up slightly as he shoved his hands into the pockets of his very expensive-looking slacks. "Historic ghost tours?"

"I've been on a lot of them, mainly along the East Coast."

"Maybe you can take me with you on one of them."

She blinked. Wait, was he asking her out? Before she could decide, his grin grew even more.

He held out a hand. A very big one. "I'm Daniel."

She held out her own, shivering at the feel of his callused palm caressing her own, at the way his hand completely engulfed hers. "Kathryn."

Something sparked between them at that moment and she knew he felt it too, because she could see the awareness flash in his blue eyes.

It mirrored the heat that rushed through her. And she realized she didn't want to take him on a historic ghost tour, she wanted to take him home right now and have her wicked way with him.

CHAPTER FOUR

Kathryn nearly turned back around the second after she stepped inside her favorite bakery. It was within walking distance of her condo and she'd been craving their cranberry muffins this morning. But when she saw Daniel sitting at one of the little tables in the corner, her stomach tightened. She wanted to put her sunglasses back on as a sort of barrier.

But it was too late. He waved at her and she of course waved back, feigning a calmness she didn't feel at all. She hadn't slept well last night—every little noise had woken her. She'd already been on edge after seeing him yesterday—and the events of last night had completely screwed up her equilibrium. And now to run into him at her favorite place? What was he even doing on this side of town? He lived in a high-rise downtown, whereas she lived in a small community filled with mostly elderly people. Her grandmother had left her the condo when she passed away and it was filled with a lot of wonderful memories. Plus it was quiet and she liked it.

Daniel stood and motioned for her to come over. And...it appeared as if he already had a couple cranberry muffins. Was he a mind reader now?

Unable to stop the frown as she approached his table, she said, "Hey, I'm surprised to see you here."

"Well I can admit to ulterior motives. I was hoping to run into you this morning."

Well, at least he was being honest. Her gaze flicked down to the muffins. "How do you feel about sharing your food?"

He snickered and sat back down so she sat across from him. Then he slid the little plate across to her. "They're all yours."

She narrowed her gaze even as she snagged one of the muffins. "You don't even like cranberry."

"But you do."

"You're pretty sneaky, showing up like this." And pushing her weakness on her—carbohydrates and yummy goodness.

"I took a chance coming here. I know you used to stop by on Saturday mornings. I already ordered your favorite drink too—a cinnamon tea latte. I told the barista to start making one if a pretty redhead joined me."

"Very, very sneaky," she said, and laughed despite the tension in her shoulders. "Clearly this isn't a chance meeting. So what's going on?" she asked, only pausing as the woman from behind the counter brought her a drink and set it in front of her with a smile. "Thank you," she murmured and looked at Daniel once they were alone again. There were people in line, but almost everyone was sitting outside at the patio tables. Only one other couple sat a few tables away, giving them a decent amount of privacy.

"To start, I know I should have called, but I didn't think you'd answer." He paused, watching her.

"I might not have."

"That's what I thought. And screw it, I needed to clear the air. One day we were together and then we were just over without warning. Last night you said something that's been bothering me. You said that I thought you were after me for my money. Why would you think that?"

This was the exact conversation she didn't want to have. She could admit that money was a sore spot for her. Her parents had argued about it for most of her childhood. Her father had continuously accused her mother of only wanting to be with him for his money until finally her mother had left him and gotten full custody of Kathryn and her two brothers.

The divorce had been the best thing that had happened to her parents because they'd been able to finally start raising their kids without all the yelling and dysfunction. They'd turned into completely different people. Better people.

"Do you remember the day I ended things with you?" she asked quietly. Clearly he wasn't giving up on this conversation, so she was going to just deal with it.

He nodded, his expression darkening.

"I don't know how much you remember about that day, but I was supposed to meet you in your office before we headed out to dinner. You were running late so your assistant had me wait in your office. And…I saw something on your desk. I was *not* snooping," she added. "The paper was literally right on your desk in front of my face and the file had my name on it in big, bold print. It was a whole file about me with a little sticky note that had the words 'gold digger' underlined three times." She felt her cheeks flush in pain and anger even as a rush of ice slid through her veins. She felt exactly as she had that day when she'd seen the file with her entire life just laid out in black and white.

He stared at her in shock.

"I wasn't looking for it," she reiterated. "But it doesn't matter. It was pretty clear you'd done some research on me. And I have no idea why you thought I was a gold digger. I also hate that word, for the record, but anyway, that's why I ended things." She shrugged and tore off the top of the muffin. She wasn't hungry anymore but managed to chew and swallow it regardless.

He stared for another long moment. "I don't know what you're talking about. I did have someone look into you when we first started dating. Technically before—"

"Wait, before?" She pushed the muffin away now, unable to even pretend to eat.

He cleared his throat. "I have to be careful. Not just because of money, but because of people who try to insinuate themselves in my life for other things as well. So yeah, Jerry looked into you, but he never called you a gold digger."

"It was in your handwriting." She knew his handwriting because he'd often left her cute little notes to find in the morning when he had to get up early for work. They hadn't been living together, not technically, but they might as well have been for all the nights they'd spent together. Which had been *all* of them. They'd alternated weeks, one at her place, then the next at his. She'd even cleared out a spot in her small closet—and he'd given her half of his giant one.

"Bullshit."

Anger surged through her. "I know what I saw. It's not like I took a picture of it or anything, so I don't have proof, but it was there. I saw it with my own eyes. And I really don't want to talk about it anymore."

"That's why you ended things with me?" His jaw tightened.

She nodded. "If you'd done, like, a simple background check or something, I obviously would have understood, but that file was a thick binder. And that note…" *Ugh.* She didn't even want to think about it anymore. When she'd seen it, it had been like all their time together had been a lie, as if she hadn't known him at all.

"Did you look at the file?"

"No. I saw the top page and the sticky note and I wanted to throw up."

"I remember you bailed early that night saying you didn't feel well."

"I wasn't lying. I *didn't* feel well."

"Look, the 'file' on you is like two pages. Not a binder full of information. I feel like a dick even admitting it now, but yeah, there was some information on your financials in it. It was very basic stuff. I just…I really liked you when we met. And I've been burned in the past."

Yeah, she knew he had, which was why it wasn't necessarily the file itself but that awful note that had changed everything for her. She shifted in her seat, wanting to believe him. But she knew what she'd seen.

"I'm sorry about the file," he continued. "I'm sorry for whatever you saw. I'm sorry that you got hurt. No, that's wrong, I'm sorry I inadvertently hurt you," he clarified. "But I never, ever wrote a note calling you that. And I really miss you," he finally murmured.

Oh, God. "I miss you too," she blurted without meaning to. It was true anyway. She'd missed him for two long months and he seemed so damn sincere. Which just served to confuse her even more. She'd seen that note. Maybe...she'd jumped to conclusions? But no. That damn thing had been underlined three times.

A long, awkward pause stretched between them so she picked up her drink, sipping on it because she wasn't sure where to go from here.

"So what's going on with this whole mugging and someone trying to attack you at your condo?" he asked, shifting directions.

Inwardly she breathed out a sigh of relief. Talking about that was much better than talking about the two of them. Especially since there wasn't a "them" anymore, and she didn't think there could be after that note. "I don't really know what to say. You heard everything last night. It's just bad luck."

He frowned, and somehow he looked even more handsome, which was ridiculous. It wasn't fair that he was so effortlessly put together. "I don't like it."

Maybe the subject change wasn't the best thing after all. Daniel could go into super overprotective mode, and he was worse than her brothers. "Well, I don't like it either. But I'm being smart about it." She cleared her throat. "So how's your sister?"

"She's been really busy the last month," he said.

"Really?"

He nodded. "Yeah, why?"

"We've been texting, but she's been totally unavailable and I thought… Honestly, I thought maybe she was blowing me off because you and I broke up." And that hurt.

He snorted at that. "Sienna told me that she wanted to keep you after the breakup, and trade me in."

Kathryn let out a startled burst of laughter and took a sip of her drink. Being with him like this now brought up far too many memories, far too many emotions she wanted to ignore. Things between them had been so great, so easy. Until she'd found that stupid note and it had fed into every single one of her insecurities.

They were from two different worlds, and to learn that he thought she was a gold digger had shaken her. He denied it and she wasn't sure what to think now. "I'm sure she didn't mean it."

He snorted again. "I wouldn't bet money on that. Look, I asked her about you being engaged."

She blinked. "What?"

"Yeah. I was annoyed that she hadn't told me about it and she was surprised. So if she says anything, sorry about that."

"Oh…ah, it's not a problem." Clearly he didn't realize that she'd been behind the job at his place. And even though she wanted to tell him, she didn't want to talk about her personal life with him.

Or more specifically, her lack of one.

CHAPTER FIVE

Normally Daniel didn't go into the office on Saturdays unless it was an emergency, but he'd scheduled an appointment with the tech company that had done a sweep of security at the new building he'd recently acquired. This was the only day that had worked well for both of them.

He stepped out of his office when he heard the elevator doors ding softly. He'd told security to send this guy directly up and his assistant wasn't here today.

As Tony Domínguez stepped out of the elevators, Daniel nodded politely at him as he strode across the waiting area directly to him. "Thanks for meeting me on a Saturday."

"No problem." In khakis, a plain button-down shirt and loafers, Tony was dressed casual today.

"I've got coffee and water and can probably find some snacks if you're hungry." There should be a bunch of snacks in the kitchen for meetings.

Tony shook his head. "I'm good. But thank you anyway."

Daniel had only had coffee that morning before Kathryn had shown up at her normal café. He felt a little bit bad about ambushing her but he'd needed to see her and clear up what had happened between them.

Now that he knew *why* she'd left him, he realized that their breakup had been because of a misunderstanding. He simply couldn't understand why there had been a sticky note on the file—one he sure as hell hadn't written. Kathryn wasn't prone to making shit up either, so he believed it had been there. And he wasn't even sure why the file had been on his desk.

It didn't make sense and he intended to get to the bottom of things. He wondered if one of her brothers had somehow set him up. They'd never really warmed up to him, but...that seemed extreme. Still...Carson, her oldest brother, had stopped by to see him a couple times before Kathryn had broken up with him. Maybe... *Hell.* He was going to figure this out later.

"I assume you already looked at the email I sent," Tony said as he sat in the plush chair in front of Daniel's desk.

He rounded the desk and sat down as well. "I did, thank you." Tony had sent him a basic outline of the very few flaws in the security. But he'd wanted to talk in person about everything that had been done to break through the first firewall yesterday before giving him the full report, something Daniel appreciated.

"This is the complete file." Tony set a binder on the desk between them. "And I'll follow up with a digital copy. Everything is broken down into categories, but basically you have a few holes in the security system, and they're all very easily fixable. More than anything, it boils down to updating certain software on-site and making sure everything is automatically updated from this point forward."

"Did the whole balloons and bubbles thing have anything to do with the security breach?" A random guy had been there at the same time Kathryn— Holy shit, was Kathryn involved? She analyzed security systems for a living, exactly what he'd hired Tony to do for him. No...she went in and evaluated security programs directly with the IT and security people. But what if she had been involved?

Was that why she'd been at the building yesterday? She hadn't been wearing the ring today and had seemed almost confused by the mention of a fiancé. Had the whole wedding planner meeting thing just been a front?

When he realized that Tony was talking, he forced his mind off the sexy redhead and focused.

"Yes. He worked with a partner who got access to another floor and used a hole in their security to infiltrate yours. Since both companies are on the same intranet, it was easy enough for her. Easy is a relative term, because she's very talented. The details are all in the report."

Her? "Does Kathryn Irish by chance work for you?"

The man's eyes widened, but only for a second. "As a rule, I don't include the names of my employees in the reports—because I've had clients try to poach my contractors—but yes, she does contract work for me. And she's the one who infiltrated your system, something you must already know."

So she *wasn't* engaged. She'd been using that as a cover to get to the eighth floor. And now that he thought about it, she actually hadn't confirmed that she was engaged anyway. She'd used deflective language. Not to mention he hadn't seen any signs at her place of a man. No clothes, shoes, no pictures. And she hadn't been wearing that huge ring this morning either.

The tight band of tension eased inside him and he felt like he could finally breathe for the first time in two days. "Good to know." Somehow his voice came out calm when he felt anything but. *Kathryn is single.* There wasn't a damn reason they shouldn't be together.

"You know her?" Tony asked.

He lifted his shoulder casually. "I've tried to hire her on full-time, more than once, but she always turns me down." Which was true. When they'd been together, he'd offered her a job—at a location he didn't work at—and she'd turned him down. She'd been right to, of course.

Tony laughed at that. "She likes doing contract work. I've offered her a full-time job myself as well. I think she likes making her own schedule, and her rates are through the roof. She's worth it of course, and I think she knows she would be making less if she worked directly for me. I simply can't offer her enough incentives to come on full-time when the top companies are fighting for her attention." He shrugged.

Yep, Kathryn was incredible, in more ways than one. And as soon as this meeting was over, Daniel intended to confront her about everything. Now that he understood why she'd left, now that he knew she was single, he wasn't wasting another day without trying to win her back. "Thank you again for all of this. I'll review it all in-depth and make sure my security team does as well. If I have any questions, I'll let you know."

They talked for a few more minutes before Tony left and Daniel flipped the binder open, scanning over the contents. What Kathryn and her partner had done had been very smart, and if he hadn't known her on a personal level and stopped to converse for those few moments, she would have been in and out of the building even more quickly than she had been.

Damn, she was good.

And now he needed to make things right with her, to win her back. He'd never stopped loving her. When people talked about the one that got away—he didn't want that to be him. He'd known from practically the first date with Kathryn that she was the one for him.

He rubbed a hand over his face, feeling off-kilter. His life was neat and organized, but then Kathryn had blown into it and tossed everything into disarray.

For the last two months he hadn't been living, he'd been going through the motions, in denial about his broken heart. He'd been going to work, making money and coming home. Sure, he went to required functions when he had to, but that was about it, and he never enjoyed them. His brother and sister had both called him out on his bullshit, but he hadn't had enough energy to do anything other than just exist.

He pulled out his cell and made a call, determined to fix things with Kathryn. Starting now.

CHAPTER SIX

Kathryn scratched Mr. Twinkles under his chin, grinning at the way he cuddled up to her. She always hated leaving him because he punished her when she came back, ignoring her completely until she fed him or gave him a treat.

Typical cat.

"I promise to bring you a treat when I get home," she said as she stood, as if he understood her.

Which she was pretty certain he did.

The white, black and orange calico cat with the twinkly eyes—hence the name Mr. Twinkles—who'd stolen her heart a year ago simply sniffed imperiously at her. Then he turned his back and swished his tail as he jumped onto the floor and plopped right down in a patch of sunshine. Yeah, he would be completely fine while she was gone.

She had a meeting with a headhunter today who swore he just wanted to talk to her about a contract job, and she really wanted to believe him. But headhunters contacted her monthly, sometimes biweekly, trying to lure her away from her actual contract work to settle down with a regular nine-to-five job. But she liked the freedom of what she did and liked being her own boss. It was still very much a man's world, especially in her line of work—and she did not want to get pigeonholed into a crappy job. Maybe one day she would change her tune, but not now.

The guy had just contacted her last night, on a Sunday no less, but his credentials were good so she decided to meet up with him and see if he had anything real to offer.

She wished she'd had more time to research this new company but she'd gone out with some friends for lunch yesterday, had yoga class and then book club—which had also included some wine time—and she hadn't had time.

Twenty minutes later here she was, wearing her rainbow sparkly sneakers, dark jeans and a T-shirt that said *Book Nerd* with glasses replacing the o's. She never dressed business casual for these things, even though she was meeting in a high-rise downtown. In the beginning of her career she had, but then she'd realized that none of the security nerds like her dressed to fit in. She'd passed that point in her career and she did not have to impress anybody.

If anything, they had to impress her. And she knew it sounded arrogant, but if she'd been a dude, it would be called confidence. So she ignored the surprised look—and quick sweep of Kathryn's attire—by the administrative assistant when she approached the front desk on the fifteenth floor. The woman's demeanor instantly changed when she told her she was Kathryn Irish.

Then the pretty blonde straightened and gave her a winning smile straight out of *Dentistry Today*. "Of course, Ms. Irish, please follow me. May I offer you something to drink? Cinnamon tea latte, cucumber water?"

She frowned at the cinnamon tea latte comment, since it was her favorite. Maybe this headhunter had done his homework. "The latte would be great, thank you."

The woman briskly nodded and hurried out on heels that looked painful to walk in.

That was one of the reasons Kathryn liked working for herself. She made the dress code and she was convinced that heels had been created by a demon.

Instead of sitting down, she strode to the bank of windows overlooking downtown and smiled at the sight. She loved the Florida coast and was glad her entire family lived here—even if her middle brother was off on some assignment. The city had always seemed so big until recently. After she and Daniel had broken up, she'd found herself avoiding places they'd gone together out of fear that she'd run into him. Because apparently she was a big ole chickenshit.

When the door opened she turned, ready to politely greet Ryan Richards, and froze for all of a second when she saw Daniel striding in, wearing another custom suit and a tie she'd actually bought him.

"Oh my God, Daniel, are you that hard up for a date that you're ambushing me now?" she snapped out before she could stop herself. She was annoyed that he was surprising her like this. *Again.* "I think we're past the point of stalking now."

Annnnnnnd that was when she saw two people behind him—a man she assumed was Ryan, the headhunter, and Daniel's pretty assistant, Nicole, who was staring at Kathryn in shock. She blinked those big blue eyes at her, looking a bit like a deer in headlights.

Kathryn winced, ready to backtrack, but to her surprise Daniel threw his head back and laughed. "Why don't you guys give us a second?" he said to the other two before very politely ushering them out. He shut the door with a soft snick and turned to face her.

"What's going on?" she demanded, annoyed.

"First of all, I'm not hard up for a date, because I'm not looking. You ruined me for other women."

She stared at him, surprised by the ridiculous statement. She'd *seen* him in the society pages more than once since she'd ended things with him. Including something this morning with a brunette knockout—which was part of the reason she'd blurted out something so rude.

"Second of all, I want to offer you a job. A contract job," he said, holding up a hand when she went to interrupt him. "I know you won't work for me directly. But I just bought a new company and I trust your judgment. I knew if I called you to one of my offices, you wouldn't answer. So I set this up with an associate of mine who's letting me use this conference room."

"You can't know that for sure." Chances were, she wouldn't have answered, but still.

"Yeah, well, I was playing the odds."

She sniffed once before approaching the conference table and sitting down. "I guess now you'll never know."

He must've taken that as a good sign because he sat across from her. "I swear this is just business. But if you agree to go on a date with me, then—"

"Noooooo, no dating talk." Still, the way he looked at her got those butterflies in her stomach going. Why couldn't she be immune to him? It was so much harder because he seemed so sincere about everything.

"Okay. For now anyway." He leaned down and pulled something out of his briefcase and slid it across to her.

When she looked inside the bag and saw a toy for her cat she smiled despite herself. "What is this, bribery?"

He shrugged, a far too wicked grin playing on his too handsome face. "I've missed Mr. Twinkles."

"He's missed you too," she said grudgingly. Her traitorous cat, who didn't warm up to anybody but her—the cat who gave the cold shoulder to even her best friend and her brothers—had practically attacked Daniel with cuddles the first time they'd met. Mr. Twinkles had curled up in his lap and meowed until he'd gotten his fill of behind-the-ear scratches. That cat was shameless. "Fair warning, I'm going to give him this toy and tell him it's from me."

This brought on another laugh from Daniel. "That's fair. So…do you want to look at the job details? I know I sprung this on you, but I really do want your expertise."

It warmed her from the inside out that he respected what she did, and getting a job with him would be really good for her portfolio. Sure, she had people knocking down the door trying to get her to work for them, but doing something for Daniel MacArthur? Yeah, this would look really good. She couldn't appear too eager, however. "I'm listening."

He quickly outlined everything for her, and as he wrapped up, he said, "For the first week, you'll be located out of my main building because I want you to run distance diagnostics. But after that you'll transfer to the new building and go from there."

She nodded and then quoted him her price. It was double what she normally charged but he didn't bat an eye.

Damn, maybe she needed to raise her rates.

"I'll have my assistant draw up a contract," he continued. "I just need to know when you can start."

"Well, as I'm pretty sure you know, I just finished a contract." Tony had shot her a text this morning letting her know that Daniel MacArthur was aware of her involvement in the last job and had been impressed by her work.

He gave her a slow grin. "I didn't realize it at the time, but yeah, I did once I talked to Tony."

"Sorry about that," she murmured, feeling a little guilty. But only a little. She could have told him that she wasn't engaged but then she would have had to explain why she'd been wearing a big ring. And that hadn't been her place, not when he'd hired Tony.

"So you're not actually engaged?" he asked, even though it was clear he knew the answer.

"No. And I'm kind of surprised you thought I would be engaged two months after we broke up." The relationship had meant a whole lot more to her than that. Clearly he hadn't had any such compunction and had moved on very quickly. He'd been dating, according to what she'd seen online.

To be fair she'd gone on a couple dates too. They'd been incredibly crappy dates, but dates nonetheless. Mainly because her friends had set her up and pushed her into it. She'd thought it would help her move on from Daniel. Of course it hadn't worked.

"I..." He cleared his throat, then turned at a soft knock on the door.

After opening it, he spoke quietly to the others and as he did, the woman from before walked in with her latte. "I'm so sorry, I would've brought this sooner but the door was shut and I didn't want to interrupt."

"Don't worry about it, I really appreciate this," Kathryn said, smiling.

"Of course. Is there anything else I can get you? Some snacks? We've got anything you can imagine."

She shook her head once as Daniel popped his head back in. "I'll be right back with the contract. If there's anything in it you don't like, or if you want your attorney to look over it, it doesn't need to be signed today."

"It depends how detailed the contract is, but if it's industry-standard then we should be fine." Usually she let her attorney look at everything but deep down she knew Daniel wouldn't screw her. And she'd read enough of these things that she had a pretty good eye for what to look for. As long as there weren't eighty-four pages of fine print, they should be okay.

He simply nodded and ducked back out again. The woman did the same, leaving Kathryn alone. Suddenly the room seemed bigger without him in it. He'd always had that effect, a sort of larger-than-life thing that made people gravitate toward him. Herself included. He didn't even seem to realize it most of the time. Being around him, even in a business setting, was messing with her head. She kept thinking about how damn sincere he'd seemed when she'd told him about that note, about the file she'd seen. It was hard to believe he was that good of a liar and really, what would be the point? He could get any woman he wanted.

Needing to get her mind off him, she pulled her cell phone out of her purse and realized she had a missed call from Detective Mendoza. As she listened to his voicemail, a lead ball settled in her gut.

"What's that look for?" Daniel asked as he stepped back into the room. Alone. She guessed the headhunter wasn't needed anymore—clearly Daniel had used the guy to get her here.

She tucked her phone away. "Nothing."

"I know that look. Come on, what's going on?"

She sighed. "I got a message from Detective Mendoza. He just wants me to come down to the station."

Daniel straightened. "Did he get a break in the case?"

She shrugged, not wanting to talk about it with him. Because if she did, then he'd be even more involved in her life. She was supposed to be getting over him. At that thought, she snorted at herself. She was such a liar—if she wanted to get over him, she wouldn't have taken this job. She would have walked out of the conference room and never looked back. Ugh, she was such a fool.

Even though she told herself to keep quiet, she said, "He wants me to look at a lineup of suspects from the mugging."

"Let's go now," he said, just taking over in that way of his.

"Daniel—"

"If he called, it's got to be important."

She stared at him. "Don't I need to go over the contract stuff?"

"I'm not worried about it. We can deal with it later. I'll have Nicole email it to you. Come on." He stood, holding the door open for her, as if the situation was settled.

She wanted to argue with him, but a very small part of her liked the idea of him coming with her to the police station. Even though she knew the mugging and near attack were coincidences, the two things had really shaken her—especially the masked man at her condo complex. Her place was so quiet, and as far as she knew there had never been anything other than extremely petty crime there. As in, bikes or potted plants getting stolen.

"You're kind of a bulldozer," she muttered as she reached the door.

"And you're kind of adorable."

Her stomach flipped over at his words. What the hell was he trying to do to her today? He'd told her he wanted to go on a date with her, that she was adorable, that she'd ruined him for other women. She couldn't deal with any of this, this…blunt honesty!

Gah. She simply needed to deal with one thing at a time and right now that was apparently looking at a lineup of potential mugging suspects.

Not obsessing about her ex-boyfriend.

CHAPTER SEVEN

Daniel was in full-on overprotective mode as he and Kathryn entered the police station. To his disappointment, her brother, Carson Irish, was waiting for her right in the busy lobby.

He and the detective were pretty close in size but Carson was broader. With his buzzed haircut and tattoos peeking out from his neckline, he looked like a street brawler more than a detective. He eyed Daniel coolly, even as he pulled Kathryn into a big hug. And when he looked at his sister, his expression completely softened.

"Hey, little bit, what's the douche doing here?" he asked, even though Daniel was standing two feet away.

Kathryn gasped slightly and nudged him in the stomach. "Be nice," she ordered, but there was absolutely no heat behind her words. Once upon a time, she would've actually been annoyed at Carson, but apparently she wasn't feeling the love for Daniel right now.

That was okay. He was going to make things right. He was in this for the long run and he wasn't letting her go. Not this time.

"Good to see you too," Daniel said mildly.

Carson just grunted at him and slid an arm around his sister's shoulders before tossing Daniel a dark look.

Annoyed that he didn't have the right to touch Kathryn, not even to hold her hand, he strode after them. They moved across the lobby and through the bullpen, a cluster of desks in an open space, before stepping into a long hallway. Carson stopped them a few doors down and motioned to it.

"I can't go any farther with you, and neither can Daniel. Just take your time," he said to Kathryn, who nodded.

She glanced back at Daniel and gave him a small smile. "Thanks for coming with me." Then she nudged Carson and ordered him to be nice. Again.

As she stepped into the room, no doubt to look at the lineup, he hated that he couldn't go with her. That he couldn't support her.

"What the hell are you doing here, MacArthur?" Carson asked, practically snarling now that they were alone. The thin veneer he'd put on earlier was completely gone.

If Kathryn had told her brother about that damn note, it was no wonder Carson seemed to hate him now. "What does it look like?"

"You have no business being with my sister."

"I'm not having this conversation with you." Especially since now he was wondering if Carson had been behind that note. "So what happened? You guys find who mugged her?"

Carson's shoulders were still bunched tight, but he leaned against the wall and crossed his arms over his chest. "Kathryn went on a date with some guy a month ago and apparently he and this guy he works with target women to rob them. It's petty shit but they're fairly organized, and in my opinion it's only a matter of time before it gets more violent. Mendoza wanted her in here to look at a lineup, see if she recognized the mugger."

"She was on a date with someone?" he asked, even though he should be focusing on so many other things.

Carson's mouth lifted up ever so slightly, a dark glint in his eyes. "Yep. And it's not the only one she's been on since she tossed your sorry ass over."

He took a steadying breath so he wouldn't punch a detective in the police station. Because even as good as his lawyers were, he didn't think they'd get him out of that. "So the mugger wasn't wearing a mask, but the guy from her condo was?"

"Yeah, I know. But these guys have followed up with more muggings. Assholes." Carson frowned, then dismissed Daniel as he pulled his phone out and started texting. "They both better go away for a long time," he finally muttered, tucking his phone away.

"How sure are you that this is the guy who was harassing her?" Daniel asked.

"Four women have ID'd him so far. These guys targeted women from their gym so there's a common denominator here, which made it easy for us to track them. Dumbasses," he muttered in disgust. "If only all criminals made it this easy."

Surprised that Carson had actually told him so much, Daniel simply grunted in agreement and leaned against the opposite wall, shoving his hands in his pockets as he waited for Kathryn to exit.

He also tried not to obsess over the fact that she had apparently been on dates. As in plural. He hadn't been able to even look at another woman since her. He'd gone to a couple work functions but the women he'd brought had been friends, someone looking for a plus-one to make the night more bearable. Something he understood. It was so much easier to fend off people when you had a "date."

When Kathryn stepped out of the room minutes later, everything else fell away as he focused on her. "Are you okay?" He stepped forward, ignoring her brother completely.

"I'm good." She smiled at him and the sight of it hit him right in the solar plexus. Damn, he'd missed her smiles. Missed waking up to her every morning. He'd even missed her needy cat, Mr. Twinkles. Who, okay, he really liked. But the name Mr. Twinkles was kind of ridiculous.

"Did you recognize anyone?" Carson asked.

She nodded. "I don't think I'm supposed to talk about it with you though."

Her brother laughed lightly and kissed the top of her head. "Look, I gotta go, we just got a suspect pulled in for another case. But I'll see you at Sunday dinner." Before he left, he shot another dark look at Daniel. "Hopefully I won't be seeing you anytime soon."

"I'm sorry about him," she murmured as her brother hurried down the hallway in the opposite direction.

He lifted a shoulder. "I've got a sister myself." And if Carson thought Daniel had labeled his sister as a gold digger, then Daniel understood why the man was pissed at him. Unless he'd planted that note—then screw him.

"You're being very accommodating about all this."

"It's not about me right now and I'm sorry you're dealing with any of this at all."

She gave him a strange look but didn't respond, simply motioned that they should head out.

At that moment, walking right next to her, he'd never felt more disconnected from her. And he hated that.

But he couldn't believe it would be this way forever. If she needed time to trust him again, he'd give it to her.

* * *

Once they were in Daniel's car, Kathryn laid her head against the headrest.

"Do you want to tell me what happened in there?" There was real concern in his voice.

"The guy who mugged me worked with some guy I went on a date with. They're both scumbags apparently. And he's actually been arrested on a bench warrant from another county so he'll be going to jail and charged with crimes that have nothing to do with me or any of his other victims here. They have a ton of evidence against the guy and it doesn't look like it's going to trial at all. Not if he agrees to a slightly shorter sentence. His partner is being charged with a bunch of conspiracy stuff too. They'll go away for at least eight years, probably longer."

"Both guys, you're sure?"

"Yes. The one who did the actual mugging will serve more time but they're not cutting a real deal for either of them. If they agree to do their time without the waste of a trial, it'll shave off a few years, but not by much. Bastards," she muttered.

"Agreed." He cleared his throat and she could feel the tension rise in the vehicle. "So…you've been dating?"

She glanced out the window, looking at the cars as they passed by. "Yeah." And it was weird to talk to him about it. She sure didn't want to talk or think about *him* dating.

"How are your brothers doing?" he asked, shifting gears. "You know, besides hating me right now?"

That pulled a laugh out of her and she turned to look at him as he drove expertly through traffic. "They're good. Carson is busy as always and Colm is out of town for work now. What about your brother?"

"On vacation."

She blinked. "Seriously?"

"Yep. I'm as surprised as you," he said dryly.

She laughed lightly. Brodie was so serious, even compared to Daniel. He owned his own security firm and did a lot of work for a local billionaire. "Good for him. He deserves the break."

Daniel shot her a look.

"What?"

"Nothing. He's asked about you… He misses you too. My whole family does."

Oh…hell. Clearing her throat, she looked away again, unsure how to respond to that. Thankfully Daniel didn't push her more. Instead, he turned the radio on low as they cruised through the throng of traffic.

And by the time they made it back to her condo, she felt more at ease and was glad that he'd driven her. She was surprised, however, when she saw her vehicle in her spot already. She'd planned to grab a rideshare later and just pick it up.

"I had your vehicle delivered so you wouldn't have to deal with getting it later."

She blinked once. "How'd you even get my keys?"

"I still had that spare from before—I swear I forgot about it until now."

Well, she didn't think he was going to steal her car. Not when he had much more expensive ones than hers. "That was very thoughtful, thank you." Daniel had always been thoughtful, so it wasn't exactly a surprise.

He parked and rounded the front of the vehicle, pulling open her door before she'd even unstrapped.

"Thanks," she murmured again. If he was a giant jerk it would make all of this a whole lot easier. Now she was confused, plain and simple. "You don't have to walk me to my door."

He simply shot her a look with raised eyebrows before falling in step with her. And as they reached her door, he turned to her and said, "I think I've made it pretty clear, but I want to put it out there. I haven't been dating since you. I don't want to date anyone but you. I want another chance."

Even at the sincerity in his voice, she snorted softly.

His eyes narrowed. "What?"

"I don't like it when people lie to me."

"You mean like telling someone they're engaged when they're not?"

She felt her cheeks heat up but she lifted a shoulder. "Technically I never told you I was engaged. You made assumptions based on what you saw and I simply didn't correct you."

His lips curved up ever so slightly. "Fine, that's fair enough. Look, I never wrote a note calling you a gold digger. Yes, I had to look into you a little bit based on past experiences. I would think that was something you could understand."

"I do understand *that*." She'd seen that note in his handwriting—but he seemed so damn sincere. He also seemed sincere about not dating and she knew what she'd seen online. But she also knew that those gossip sites lied. She was too embarrassed to tell him she'd been sorta stalking him online so didn't bring up what she'd seen. "My brother looked into you a little bit too," she murmured. "Before our first date."

He blinked once before that grin was back in place. "I'm not actually surprised."

"He likes to make sure I'm not dating losers."

"So what happened with the last guy?" His tone was dry.

"I didn't tell him, but in hindsight I probably should've. It would have saved me a headache. And a mugging—and likely a lunatic trying to attack me at my condo." At that thought she wrapped her arms around herself and glanced over the balcony at the parking lot.

"You really haven't been dating?" she asked, wanting to believe him.

"No. Though in full disclosure, I did take a woman to a business dinner thing recently. We both went as each other's plus-ones as a favor. She gets sick of being hit on and I do too, to be honest. It made things easy. We acted as each other's buffer. And…I think I took a friend to something last month too. Again, just as buffers. That's it."

A sharp sense of relief slid through her. "I believe you. And…" Maybe she was going to regret this, but, "I'll go on a date with you. *One* date." Until that stupid note, she'd been so secure in what she and Daniel had together. She was going with her gut right now and hoping it didn't fail her.

"Tomorrow night?" he asked immediately.

She laughed lightly. "I think I can manage that."

He watched her for a long moment, his blue eyes searching. "Why did you say yes?"

"Because I don't think you lied to me. I don't think you *intentionally* lied to me anyway. I don't know, you just seem really sincere." And she'd also missed him a whole lot. He'd always been so thoughtful—leaving sweet little notes for her every morning, not pushing her to go public with their relationship, always having her tea ready in the morning, paying attention to the little things—actually listening to her. He'd been the perfect boyfriend.

Though the word boyfriend didn't really fit him because he was all man. And if she didn't try, she knew she'd regret it. She'd ended things so abruptly and had never gotten a sense of closure.

Reaching out, he cupped her cheek, and for a long moment she thought he would kiss her. Time seemed suspended as they stood there, watching each other. But he didn't make a move. "Tomorrow, seven o'clock," he rasped out, so much need and hunger in his voice and expression.

"I'll be here," she whispered, her voice as unsteady as his. She was disappointed he hadn't made a move to kiss her, but that was most definitely for the best. Because if they started kissing, she wasn't so sure she would want to stop.

CHAPTER EIGHT

Daniel closed his laptop as his younger brother stepped into his office. He smiled, glad to see Brodie back from vacation. "Hey, how was the vacation? Catch any fish?"

Brodie raised his eyebrows. "Are you...in a good mood?" he whispered the last part like an obnoxious jackass.

Rolling his eyes, he stood and rounded his desk. "Come on, how was the vacation?"

"All right, who are you and what have you done with my brother?" Brodie grinned, his face more tanned than normal as he strode in wearing jeans and a T-shirt with a familiar surf brand on it. He looked a lot more relaxed than Daniel had seen him in a while. Normally he was in sharp suits and had a "don't mess with me" expression firmly in place.

"Ha, ha." He pulled Brodie into a tight hug.

"I'm just saying, it's the first time in a while you haven't snarled at me."

Daniel snorted. "You're full of it. And you're in a good mood too."

"So?"

"So...what? You gonna tell me about your vacation or not?" He leaned against the edge of his desk as Brodie watched him expectantly.

"I caught a bunch of fish, caught up on reading, and didn't talk to almost anyone for two weeks. It was amazing."

Daniel knew his brother had basically fallen off-grid, like he often did when he took a couple days away. But Brodie had been gone two weeks this time. Clearly it had been good for him. "Good for you."

"Now it's your turn. What's going on with you? You're not the sad sack you were a couple weeks ago."

"She's going out with me tonight," he said simply. And he didn't need to specify who she was either. He could admit that he was nervous too, which was unfamiliar territory for him. But Kathryn had always made him feel like a horny teenager with no moves.

Brodie's eyes widened slightly. "Good for you. Hope you guys get it right this time."

Yeah, so did he. He pressed his intercom. "Nicole, reschedule my four thirty and five o'clock. Sorry I didn't let you know earlier." He'd been consumed with working on contracts and had forgotten.

There was a short pause, then, "Of course, sir."

He looked at his brother again. "What are you doing here anyway? Not that I'm not happy to see you."

"I was on my way home and thought I'd see if you wanted to grab a couple beers, but I know the answer is no."

He thought about trying to squeeze it in before meeting Kathryn, but there was no way. "Why don't you call Sienna, see what she's up to?" He needed to check on his sister too. She'd been so damn cagey lately when he asked her what she was doing.

"Already tried. She answered the phone, said she just wanted to make sure it wasn't an emergency, then hung up on me." Brodie grinned slightly.

"So I'm the second choice? That's cold, man." He grabbed his laptop case off his desk and motioned that he was going to head out.

"My plan was always to ask both of you."

"Let's plan something this week, then," he said as they stepped into the outer office. He nodded once at his assistant, who was intensely focused on her computer screen. "Nicole, you can leave once you've rescheduled those meetings. I think we can afford to take off early today."

She looked surprised but then smiled. "Of course, thank you."

"Hopefully you don't screw things up with Kathryn again," Brodie bluntly said as they headed for the elevators.

"Not this time. I'm gonna put a ring on her finger." He already had the ring—had bought it a week before she'd ended things. Even when she'd broken up with him, he hadn't been able to get rid of it.

Brodie shot him a surprised look.

He simply shrugged as he pressed the down button. He knew what he wanted. And that was Kathryn. He knew they were right together and that if he didn't lock her down, it would be the greatest mistake of his life.

"That's pretty huge. Not that I'm surprised, considering the way you moon over her," Brodie said as they stepped into the elevator.

"Did you just say the word *moon?*"

His brother lifted a shoulder. "Don't change the subject."

"Anyway, I won't be screwing this up. I've got a plan."

"You and your plans," his brother muttered, shaking his head.

"I can't wait until you fall for someone."

Now Brodie just snorted. "Not gonna happen. Not in a million years."

* * *

Daniel's breath caught in his throat as Kathryn opened her door. He'd barely had time to get home, change and get over here on time after he'd seen Brodie. Now he wished he'd made it even sooner.

She had on a green summer dress that made her emerald-colored eyes seem even brighter than normal—and it hugged her curves in all the right places. She had a light tan—probably from all her forced outdoor activities with friends—bringing out the freckles across her nose and cheeks. And when she smiled at him, her expression so open, he forgot to breathe for a moment. God, he'd missed her.

"You look stunning," he managed to get out as she stepped back to let him in.

"You look pretty good yourself."

In casual jeans and a polo shirt, he didn't even compare to her. Nothing did. He held out the small bag he'd brought for her.

"A gift on a first date?" she asked, even as she took it.

He lifted a shoulder. They'd agreed to start over and treat this like a first date but that didn't mean he wasn't bringing her something. He loved the way she smiled when she opened up any sort of gift, no matter how small. She was like a kid on Christmas.

"Want to come in for a drink? I normally don't invite first dates in, but I'll make an exception." Her grin was cheeky.

He didn't like to think of her going out on dates with anyone *but* him, but he nodded and stepped inside. Her place was the same as it had been the other night, yet there was a subtle difference from the way it had been over two months ago. All traces of him had been erased and it bothered him even if he understood why.

"Ooh, fancy British tea." Her eyes lit up as she set the bag on her kitchen countertop. "And macaroons! Thank you. I'll be getting into these later for sure." Grinning, she pulled out a bottle of red wine. "I've got wine, or Carson left some beers in my fridge last time he was here. It's the kind you like too."

"Beer's good." His gaze strayed to her nearly bare shoulders. The straps of her dress didn't cover much and all he could think about was baring more of her. Of kissing her senseless, of making her climax until she was sated and exhausted.

"You can grab it," she said as she started pouring a glass for herself. "Before we head out, do you want to sit on my patio and watch my neighbors? Unless we have reservations somewhere?"

He grinned as he pulled an ice-cold bottle from her fridge. "Neighbor watching. Definitely." Back when they'd been dating, some nights they'd sit on her back patio that overlooked the condo complex pool, and people watch. She was by far the youngest person who lived here, since the place had been left to her by her grandmother. It wasn't officially a retirement complex but ninety percent of the residents were fifty-five and older. Kathryn loved people watching and he'd found that he enjoyed it too. At least when he was with her.

"You've got some catching up to do," she said as she pushed the sliding glass door open. "Mr. Diaz is now dating Miss Cooper."

A warm breeze rolled over them, reminding him that Florida summer was soon on its way. He sat next to her, stretching his legs out on a lounge chair as she did the same. Normally she would have curled up in the same lounger as him. "What happened with Ms. Lopez?"

"Apparently she caught him cheating on her with Ms. Johnson. But that was over quickly and now he's with Miss Cooper. But I saw Miss Cooper fooling around with Mr. Gomez two nights ago."

He snickered as he glanced over at the pool area where some of the residents they were talking about were lounging, drinking and playing their radio at a higher than necessary level.

A few of them waved when they saw him, including Miss Cooper. "Daniel, darling, we've missed seeing you!" she called out, yelling across the pool to be heard. "Come visit us before you leave!"

He simply held up his beer and saluted her. As he did, Mr. Twinkles slipped outside and jumped into his lap.

"He's definitely missed you," Kathryn murmured, taking a sip of her wine and watching him over the rim of her glass.

"Just Mr. Twinkles?"

"I might've missed you a little bit."

All his muscles pulled taut at her teasing tone. "A little bit, huh?"

"Maybe more than a little bit, but you already have a large enough ego, so we're going to leave it at that."

The residual tension in his chest eased. He'd been nervous on the way over here, but as always when he was around Kathryn he just felt light and free, as if he could be his real self. He wasn't rushing to make the next deal, answering a thousand emails, going from one meeting to the next or a million other things that he had to take care of during the day. No, when he was with her, he was simply *with* her and living in the moment. She always brought out the best in him.

"So I was thinking of going to Barbie's Burgers," he said. It was a local burger joint, casual, and he knew she loved the place.

"You know the way to my heart, through burgers and beer."

He did indeed.

And tonight he was going to claim her heart once and for all.

CHAPTER NINE

Kathryn Irish was with *him* again, just sitting and enjoying drinks at her place. Somehow the cute little security nerd had lured Daniel back into chasing after her like a fool.

Men were stupid when it came to women, however. So it wasn't that much of a surprise.

But Irish had to go. It wasn't personal, it was business.

Maybe it was a *little* personal.

The woman had been prepared the other night with her pepper spray, but that wouldn't happen again. Nope.

Daniel opened the passenger door for Irish before getting into the driver's side. *What a gentleman.*

It had been impossible to put a tracker on Daniel's vehicle, since security checked his truck at work, so it would be pointless—and it might get Daniel's hackles up.

Right now it was imperative that nothing tipped Daniel off.

As Daniel steered out of the parking lot with Irish riding next to him, it wasn't difficult to keep a decent way back, weaving in and out of traffic, just going with the flow. The roads were crowded for a Tuesday night but luckily the happy couple didn't go far.

It should be easy enough to keep an eye on them—on her.

It was impossible to understand what Daniel saw in the woman. Sure, she was attractive, with pert breasts and a pretty smile, but she dressed like a college-aged girl and had no style. No elegance. She was smart, however, so maybe that was the appeal?

Too bad for Irish, the time had come to eliminate her. She should have stayed away from Daniel, should have stayed broken up. If she had, she wouldn't be right in the crosshairs.

As it was, Kathryn Irish's days were numbered, so hopefully she enjoyed what little time she had left.

CHAPTER TEN

"Thanks for dinner," Kathryn murmured as she and Daniel stood. He'd somehow wrangled a table on the back deck of the restaurant, overlooking the ocean.

A cool, salt-tinged breeze rolled over them as Daniel took her hand in his. "Let's walk on the beach before we head back."

Him taking her hand felt like the most natural thing in the world and sent butterflies launching inside her. "It's a pretty night out." And she wanted to spend more time with him. Tonight had felt familiar, as if no time had passed between them at all. That in itself was a little scary, how fast she slipped back into feeling like they belonged together.

He led them across the back patio to the wooden walkway that led to the beach. She slipped off her sandals and he did the same with his shoes, leaving them by the end of the stairs as they headed toward the shore.

The sand was cool and dry against her feet.

"I don't want to wait until the end of our date to kiss you," Daniel murmured.

"Are you assuming that you'll even get a kiss on this date?" she asked, bumping him with her hip as they trekked across the sand. Chances were, he was going to get a kiss. More than one.

"I would never assume, Miss Irish," he said. "But I am very hopeful."

A grin pulled at her mouth. "We'll see." *Liar, liar.* There was no "we'll see." It was very likely going to happen. She only had so much restraint when it came to him. And it wasn't a lot.

"You kissed me on our *other* first date," he murmured, his voice dropping a few octaves.

Oh yes, she had. Just like that, a rush of heat slid through her body, curling tight in her belly as she remembered that first kiss. He'd been looking at her mouth as if he'd wanted to eat her alive and it had set something free inside her. She'd practically attacked him then—and he'd taken over in an instant, going into what she thought of as full-on dominating Daniel mode.

That kiss had led to a little *more* than kissing, and had been totally out of character for her. But she'd never been on a date with anyone like Daniel MacArthur before either. Someone who made her feel alive and sexy and who accepted her for who she was. She'd done a little bit of digging into his past social life after he first asked her out and she was *not* the type of woman he'd seemed to date before. The women he'd been linked with were all polished and elegant and had all run in the same society circles.

Her parents had been blue collar and she'd grown up as one of the boys—and she liked it that way. She had a bunch of girlfriends now, but she was always going to be a casual, jeans-wearing kind of girl at heart. And Daniel didn't seem to mind at all, he just liked her for who she was. He never made her feel less than.

"I did get kind of crazy the first night we went out," she admitted.

"So did I."

More heat flooded her as she remembered the way he'd gone down on her, brought her to orgasm with his mouth and fingers. God, he'd been frantic to make her come. And she'd replayed that first date in her mind more than once.

As they got closer to the softly crashing waves, he tugged on her hand and they both sat in a dry patch of sand, stretching their legs out. The sand between her toes felt good, the three-quarter moon shining down on the near empty beach setting a romantic tone.

"I saw Brodie today," Daniel said into the mostly quiet. Behind them music from the restaurant carried on the wind, but other than that, the waves were the only sound. "He told me not to screw things up with you."

She laughed lightly at the mention of his younger brother. "How is Brodie? I've missed him," she said, meaning it. She'd missed the whole MacArthur clan. They were fun and loud and nothing like she'd imagined a family so wealthy would be like. Parties at his parents' house had always been a riot—which ended in savage board games where one of them usually did an awful victory dance. He let out a low sort of growl that made her laugh. "You can't be jealous."

Daniel shrugged, not answering one way or another. So she rolled her eyes.

He finally spoke. "He's good, just got back from vacation. I can't believe he actually took one. He's such a workaholic."

"Do you not hear the irony in that statement? When was the last time *you* took a vacation?"

He didn't even pause. "That getaway you and I took down to the Bahamas."

At that memory, even more heat curled through her, settling low. They'd spent almost the entire time naked or with her in a bikini. Usually just bikini bottoms because she'd gone topless the majority of the time—at his request. It had been just the two of them in a private cabana on a private beach. Like something out of a fairy tale.

"You work too hard," she murmured, leaning closer to him and feeling oddly protective of him. He needed to take better care of himself.

Surprising her, he turned slightly to face her more and reached out, cupping her cheek with one big hand.

He watched her for a long moment, the sound of the crashing waves drowning out everything but the beat of her heart. He gently stroked his thumb over her cheek, just watching her with an intensity she felt to her core.

Sitting here like this, she felt exposed and vulnerable, as if Daniel could read her every thought, every want.

Going on instinct, she shifted over and straddled him, taking both of them by surprise. She hadn't planned to make a move on him but it had been two long months. And she'd missed him so much. She wasn't quite sure what this would mean for them, but this felt like more than a first date. It felt like they were together again, even if neither of them had said anything.

"Kathryn," he groaned, wrapping his arms around her and holding her tight as he crushed his mouth to hers.

She loved the feel of his tongue teasing hers, and the way he held her so close, as if he didn't want to let her go. She rolled her hips against him, wanting to get as close as possible, wanting to ease the ache between her legs. She needed way more than this though. Over the last two months she'd masturbated so many times to memories of them, even as she'd cursed him. Tonight she didn't have to imagine anymore, she had him right here in her arms.

Suddenly Daniel's fingers clenched on her hips, stilling her as he pulled back. His chest rose and fell with his ragged breathing.

She stared at him, their semi-public surroundings rushing back to her.

"We really need to stop before we...*don't* stop."

"I know," she said, even as she rolled her hips over his erection again. Oh God, she'd missed the feel of him between her legs like this. She just hated that there was clothing between them and that they weren't somewhere private.

He groaned and laid his forehead against hers. "You make me crazy."

Yeah, well, the feeling was mutual.

The sound of people laughing in the distance brought her back to reality even more. "It probably wouldn't do to get a violation out here on the beach for public indecency," she muttered as she forced herself to roll off him.

"Your brother could get you out of it—though I'm pretty sure he'd also punch me in the face."

She laughed lightly at his dry tone. "I don't think he'd punch you. Besides, you've got some moves of your own."

He grinned. "I've got moves—that I want to show you right now."

She laughed again before he stood and pulled her up with him.

It was probably for the best. Things were moving way too fast and she needed to slow things down. She'd gotten burned so badly before and now it was clear that she was just jumping right back into things with him. Before Daniel, she'd been the queen of self-control and good decisions. Whether or not getting back together with Daniel was a bad decision remained to be seen. She just knew that she didn't want to screw things up.

He wrapped his arm around her shoulders and turned back toward the restaurant. Out of the corner of her eye, she thought she saw a flash of light, but when she looked nothing was there but the sand dunes. Probably just somebody taking a selfie.

The drive back to her condo didn't take long but her stomach was doing flip-flops by the time they reached her front door. They hadn't talked much on the drive back, but the ride had been comfortable, familiar. Which scared her a little. Everything about being with him again just felt right and she was scared that it would all get screwed up again. That she'd be right back where she'd been two months ago, crying into her ice cream and Mr. Twinkles' fur. *Bah.*

As they reached the top of her stairs, she leaned back against her front door as Daniel caged her in, his big hands next to her head, his forearms and biceps flexing.

Warmth flooded between her legs at the show of power. Seriously, the man was carved from stone. It was absolutely ridiculous how he just screamed sex appeal. Arms should not be that sexy.

He stared down at her with a familiar, hungry glint in his eyes, not saying anything. But she knew where this was leading.

Even though it took self-control she didn't realize she had, she pressed a hand to the middle of his chest and gently stilled him. She couldn't let him kiss her again.

Because if she let his lips touch hers, that self-control she was barely hanging on to? Yeah, it would be completely shredded and they would be naked inside her living room within moments. Then he'd be deep inside her while they tumbled to the floor because with the way he was watching her, she was pretty sure they wouldn't make it to the bedroom. Not the first time. Maybe not even the second.

She clenched her thighs together and pushed slightly.

He groaned but he dropped his hands and stepped back.

"No more kissing for tonight." For…reasons. She was sure she had them. Right?

"Okay. When can I take you out again?"

Her brain sort of went on the fritz as she tried to think of her schedule. She blinked. "I've got plans tomorrow and then I'm free the next night."

"I'll pick you up, same time?"

She nodded, but he still didn't step back.

"I had fun tonight," he said quietly.

"Me too."

He watched her for another long moment then groaned again, softly, and stepped back, giving her room to breathe and think again. Just like that, her brain kicked into gear, all cylinders go. It was like when she was close enough to touch him, everything just slowed wayyyy down and all she had was sex on the brain.

"Good night," she murmured.

"Good night."

Somehow she managed to make her body listen to her. Sliding her key into the lock, she hurried inside. Then she locked her door, turned off the alarm, then reset it because she knew he wouldn't leave until he heard that little telltale *beep beep beep*.

Taking a deep breath, she dropped her purse onto the kitchen countertop and shoved out a sigh. Right now she could be naked and getting an orgasm, but no, she'd had to show self-control. She groaned out loud and laid her head on the countertop, berating herself as Mr.

Twinkles wound his way in between her legs, meowing incessantly for her to pick him up.

As she scooped him up in her arms, her phone buzzed.

When she saw it was a text from Daniel, her heart rate kicked up about a thousand notches.

I'll be thinking of you tonight as I stroke myself off.

Her cheeks heated up even though he couldn't see her. They'd never really texted like this before. Yes, they'd sent flirty texts, but nothing overtly sexual. She bit her bottom lip as she stared at her phone. Mr. Twinkles continued to nuzzle his head under her chin, completely unconcerned about anything else.

Before she had time to obsess over her response, she quickly typed one back. *I'll be thinking of you as I tease my clit tonight.* Was that too bold? Too much? Not enough? Gah, she wasn't good at this. So she hit send before she could second-guess herself.

A moment later he sent her back an emoji of a cartoon fox with his tongue hanging out of his mouth and hearts above his head. She laughed aloud at the ridiculous emoji even as warmth filled her chest. Maybe tonight was the beginning of something new between them.

She'd missed him so damn much, had thought of him every single day that they'd been apart. Still, she didn't want to get ahead of herself. She didn't want to make the same mistakes her mom had made and fall for the wrong man.

She had to be smart about this, had to be careful. She didn't want to be humiliated and heartbroken again. Years ago she'd promised herself that she'd never let a man have complete power over her heart.

Unfortunately, being careful about matters of the heart was damn near impossible. Especially where Daniel MacArthur was concerned.

CHAPTER ELEVEN

Daniel couldn't stop the energy humming through him. Kathryn started at the office today to begin her diagnostics, and yeah, he was excited to see her. About the only reason he was excited on a Monday morning.

Instead of heading up to his floor, he went straight to the security floor.

They were supposed to have gone on a date Thursday, but her mom had been sick so she'd canceled on him. And then she'd ended up taking care of her mom all weekend, something he understood. He'd actually dropped off some chicken soup and got to see Kathryn for a few minutes but it wasn't the same as spending time with her. This morning she'd texted him that her mom was feeling better and she would see him soon.

He might have sent back a dirty text, which was probably inappropriate, but it wasn't like he was her boss. Not technically. She was an independent contractor and he could keep things professional. Mostly.

As he reached the security floor, he smiled when he saw her stepping off the other elevator. She had on dark jeans, heels—which surprised the hell out of him—and a fitted black jacket over a green camisole. "You look hot," he murmured.

She gave him a startled laugh. "Thanks. Is it the heels?" She lifted a foot, grinning.

"I wouldn't mind seeing you wearing only them."

Her cheeks flushed. "Just figured I'd mix it up today. So, this is weird timing, you showing up now. Did you plan it?"

He shook his head then glanced up and down the hallway. It was empty so he closed the distance to her and brushed his mouth over hers. He resisted the urge to tug her into his arms, to pin her up against the nearest wall.

She leaned into his kiss, flicking her tongue against his before quickly stepping back. Then she glanced up and down the hall as well. "I don't want people to think I got this contract job because…of whatever this is."

That gave him the perfect opening, the one he'd been waiting for. "So what is this?"

She blinked once, then shook her head. "No way. I've only had one chai this morning and it's far too early to have this kind of conversation."

"We're going to have this conversation soon." He fell in step with her as they headed down the hallway.

"Hmmm."

"You can hmm all you want, it's happening." He knew he should ease up, but he wanted it clear what they were—and he wanted exclusive. Always had.

Always would.

"So what does your day look like today?" she asked, completely ignoring his statement. She had on her security lanyard with her temporary pass around her neck.

"A few contracts to go over, a couple international conference calls, two off-site checks and some more boring stuff."

"You love this stuff."

He lifted a shoulder. He liked making money and he liked what he could do with that money. His company put a quarter of their revenue back into the community, into charities that truly needed it. His parents had both grown up poor and they'd instilled in him a need to give back as much as possible from the time he was young.

"Well, you clearly know where you're going, so I'll leave you to it," he said as they paused outside the security room door.

"You want to meet up for lunch, or will you be too busy taking over the world?"

Oh, he could think of something they could do over lunch. "Lunch. My office."

She lifted an eyebrow. "I recognize that look," she whispered. "So how about lunch at one of the local food trucks? There's a new Cuban one down here that I want to try."

"Food truck it is, but the offer to do lunch in my office stands if you change your mind. If not, I'll meet you downstairs at noon."

She nodded. "Works for me."

He resisted the urge to kiss her again and that was pretty much only because the door opened and the head of his security in this building stepped out.

Cora smiled as she looked between the both of them. "Mr. MacArthur, I didn't expect to see you today. Can I help you with anything?"

"Nope. Just walking Ms. Irish down here."

"It's nice to meet you officially in person," Cora said as she held out a hand to Kathryn. In a sharp black business suit, the tall, lean woman looked as she always did. Put together and intimidating. Her dark hair was pulled back in a twist and the only jewelry she wore was her wedding ring and diamond studs he knew that her husband had given her as an anniversary present. "I've heard great things about you."

Kathryn smiled back and he knew she was in good hands. He also knew she was going to help them extensively. So he murmured goodbye and hurried off.

By the time he made it back to his office, he'd already received eight texts from his assistant and six phone calls from other employees.

"Mr. MacArthur," Nicole said as he stepped into the office. She pushed back from her desk, and stepped around it wearing such thin stilettos he wasn't sure how she managed to walk in them. "I moved a couple of your meetings around today. I just sent the alerts to your phone."

He nodded. "Thank you. As long as I've got nothing between twelve and one, I'm fine." He normally skipped lunch, either eating in his office or using his lunch break to hit up the gym in the building.

She frowned down at her tablet. "Actually, I did schedule a phone conference for twelve thirty. I didn't realize you had anything on the books."

Neither had he until a minute ago. "Who's the meeting with?" he asked even though he knew he was going to cancel it. Meeting up with Kathryn was more important. When Nicole told him, he shook his head. "Reschedule it."

"Will do. Don't forget you have that gala on Thursday."

Oh, hell. "That's right."

"Did you still want me to go with you?" she asked.

Hell, he'd forgotten about that too. It was a working function and he'd needed someone to run interference. "No, take the night off." He would make sure she was still paid overtime since he'd told her to schedule the time.

She nodded. "Thank you. And I'll let the organizer know it will just be you."

"No, just leave things as they are. I'm bringing someone."

She looked surprised, but simply nodded and put something into her tablet.

Two hours later, when he received a text from Kathryn, his heart rate increased just from seeing her name on the screen. Damn, he was done for. Just absolutely done. Disappointment slid through him, however, when he read her text.

It looks like we're going over a lot of technical stuff today. Cora wants to call lunch in and since I want to make friends on my first day, I wanted to double-check with you. Rain check?

He texted back quickly. *Of course. How about dinner tonight?* Then maybe they could have that uncomfortable conversation he was dying for.

She didn't respond and he frowned.

He knew she hadn't blown him off Thursday or this weekend, but still that insecurity settled in his bones. Insecurity he'd never experienced until Kathryn. Not that she made him feel insecure in the general sense, just like he wasn't always on his game. She kept him on his toes and he liked that part, but hated being kept away from her.

Five minutes later she texted back. *I'll let you know?*

Okay, so that definitely wasn't a yes. He frowned but set his phone down and buzzed his assistant to ask if she could get the lunch meeting back on.

Hours later, and countless meetings later, Daniel had a low-grade headache by the time he shut everything down. After he checked in with security and found out that Kathryn was still on the security floor, he headed there instead of leaving.

As he reached the door to the security room, Kathryn and Cora both walked out at the same time.

Cora of course was surprised to see him, since he didn't come down here often, but Kathryn gave him a real smile he felt all the way to his core.

"Mr. MacArthur, did you need me—"

He shook his head, cutting Cora off. "No, I just wanted to talk to Ms. Irish about some things before she heads out."

She nodded. "Well, then, I'm going to leave. Night shift just got here and everything looks good. But I'm sure Kathryn will tell you everything in her end-of-the-week report." She gave Kathryn a warm smile and headed off, purse on her shoulder.

"You look exhausted," Kathryn said, then winced. "And I don't mean that in a mean way, like you look bad. Did you have a rough day?"

"Just long." A merger he was interested in had fallen through and it was the fault of no one. It was just one of those things where the timing didn't work out and he was frustrated. He liked being in control, something he could admit. And the merger would have created thousands of jobs in a community that needed it. "It's better now though." Just seeing her made everything better. "So, dinner tonight?"

She paused and he felt that knife in his gut twist.

"No pressure. I don't want you to feel like you have to have dinner with me." Especially since she was working here the next couple weeks.

She reached out and laid a hand on his forearm, her touch gentle. "I'm not blowing you off. I promise. But it was a really long day. I kind of want to go home, get into my PJs and watch Netflix. And that's not a euphemism, I really want to Netflix and chill. Literally."

He snorted. "No pressure, but if you want company, I'll join you."

She started walking down the hallway with him. "I would *love* the company. I just thought you wanted to go out. We can get takeout from that Chinese place down the street."

"Works for me. Actually, I'll pick up dinner for us on the way and meet you there so we don't even have to call it in. You know what you want?"

She grinned. "You know exactly what I want."

His mouth curved up. She never changed her order, and when he'd asked her about it she'd said that she liked what she liked, and after trying most of the menu she always kept coming back to the same thing.

"I'll pick up a bottle of wine for us, then," Kathryn said. Then she looked around at the empty hall, grabbed him by the front of his jacket and pulled him down to her for a quick, hot kiss. Breathing hard, she stepped back. "That's the last time that happens while we're at work. I just couldn't resist."

"Good, because I can barely resist you on days that end in Y." Her cheeks flushed pink and just like that his dick was hard. The weight that had been pressing on his chest all day had lifted as he headed out with her. Even though he wanted to, he resisted the urge to take her hand in his. "Oh, there's a dinner thing on Thursday night I'm supposed to go to. I know it's not your style, but if you're interested, I'd like to have you as a plus-one."

"So…that would link us publicly for sure."

"It would." He hadn't pressured her before, even though he'd wanted to. She was skittish about relationships and he'd wanted to respect that. Even if it had killed him a little inside. Now he wanted to stake a public claim.

She was silent as the elevator descended. "I'll see if Chloe has a dress I can wear," she finally said. "But yes, I'd love to go."

And just like that, he knew that things between them had changed. But he was still talking to her tonight. He wanted to know exactly where she was at, and where they stood. "Don't worry about the dress. I've got you covered."

She looked over at him, eyebrows raised. "Really?"

He nodded. He'd actually bought a dress for her for another event he'd invited her to before they'd broken up, and he hadn't been able to get rid of it. So it was hanging in his closet, a sad reminder of her.

"Should I be worried that it's low-cut and tight?"

He grinned. "You'll like it, trust me." And yeah, it was low-cut and would look sexy as hell on her.

Taking him by surprise, she grabbed his hand as they stepped out of the elevator and linked her fingers with his.

In that moment, he knew she was making a statement about them without saying a word at all. Soon he intended to claim her fully, to make sure everyone knew she was taken.

To make sure that *she* knew, without a doubt, she was the one for him. And that he wasn't letting her go.

CHAPTER TWELVE

Kathryn was so glad that Daniel had wanted to come home and relax with her. Though she knew they'd be doing more than just relaxing.

She hadn't wanted to say no to his date but she also really hadn't wanted to go out anywhere. She'd gotten information overload today at his office and was still digesting everything she'd been sifting through. When she took big jobs like this, they could be mentally draining. And she hadn't wanted to start off this new thing between them with what amounted to her lying. She wanted to start fresh—to be real and open about their relationship. First they needed to actually define their relationship, though she felt as if she'd made it clear what she wanted today.

At the sound of a knock on her door, she grinned and pulled it open.

"Did you check the peephole?" he asked as he stepped inside carrying two brown bags.

She shut and locked the door behind him. "I knew it was you."

"So that's a no."

"I'll do it next time." She should've actually checked. She knew better. It didn't matter that her mugger was in jail, there were still a whole lot of other weirdos out in the world. "Wow, that smells so good. Mainly because I didn't have to cook it."

He snickered as he set the boxes on her kitchen island top. "So how was your first day?"

She started pulling out plates and glasses for them. "Really great. There's a lot of information, more than I expected, but I know what I'm dealing with and you have a really incredible team. Something I'm sure you already know because you hired them. I'm excited to do the on-site check next week at the new building, but so far things are good. Your core security team is so sharp. Oh, and John is so adorable," she added. "I haven't seen him in ages." They'd worked together on a few jobs before he went full-time with Daniel.

Daniel frowned and she blinked.

Then she broke into a grin. "I forgot how territorial you are. What I mean is, he's adorable because his wife just had twins and he was gushing about all of them." And she was a sucker for cute baby pictures.

"I'm not territorial—just possessive of what's mine." The heated glint in his eyes, the way his voice wrapped around her, and she suddenly forgot all about the food.

Was she his? She sure felt like it. "Is there a difference between the two?"

Wordlessly he stalked around the island toward her, determination in his gaze.

"It's too soon," she whispered, even though he hadn't said a word. But she clearly read that look in his eyes.

"Why is *this* too soon?" He erased the last of the distance between them, pinning her against the countertop.

"It just is." *Wow, great response.*

"This is *our* relationship. *We* set the rules." But he stepped back, nonetheless, giving her a bit of space.

"What exactly is our relationship?" And was she being a fool by jumping straight back into something with him? She'd basically already made the decision, because after Thursday it would become common knowledge around the city that they were an item. It was a little hard to care about any sort of consequences when he was looking at her like she was the most precious thing in the world, however.

"I want to be exclusive," he said as if that was obvious.

She did too. She knew she'd agreed to start dating him but she'd never been the type of person who could date others, and she certainly couldn't date someone like Daniel *and* others at the same time. It wasn't the way she was wired. "I don't want to be with anyone else either," she whispered. "Just don't break my heart." Saying that made her feel a hundred times more vulnerable.

"Never." Reaching out he cupped her cheek, and with that small action he anchored her, made her feel more connected to him.

"How about we get dessert before dinner?" she murmured. Dessert first sounded like a great idea. The best one ever.

With that, his mouth curved up into a sexy grin before he crushed it to hers.

She was vaguely aware of her cat running off, likely to hide while they got busy. A little voice inside her told her to guard her heart, but she knew she couldn't guard it forever. She was either going to jump into this thing or she wasn't. All she knew was that she couldn't straddle the line. She had to commit or not.

Teasing her tongue against his, she molded to him, wrapping her arms around him as he pulled her close. She'd missed this, missed *him*.

For two long months, they'd been denied this.

When he grabbed her ass and started kneading it, heat flooded between her legs, hot and molten. She jumped him then, not happy with just having her arms around him. She wanted more, everything. And they needed to be naked like ten minutes ago.

He took over, lifting her up, and somehow they made it to her living room where they ended up sprawled on her much too small couch. That was okay though.

He had her clothing off in seconds, even her heels—which she'd worn today for him. "You got me naked incredibly fast."

The look he gave her was scorching. "Two months without you, Kathryn. Two. Months."

Yeah, she felt that way too. In response, she reached for the bottom button of his shirt and started working each of them free. If she was going to be naked, she wanted to feel his skin on hers. Wanted to feel him pressing her into the couch, wanted him to fill her completely as she came around him.

He let her take off his shirt but instead of letting her go for his pants he kissed her again, threading his fingers through her hair and kissing her as if he had all the time in the world.

Meanwhile she felt as if she was ready to combust underneath him. Every flick, every tease of his tongue against hers set her on fire even more.

She rolled her hips against his, the friction of his erection against her slick folds driving her crazy. She just wanted those pants gone so she could feel all of him. The stimulation wasn't quite enough even though it felt amazing.

As if he read her mind—or maybe her body language—he reached between their bodies and cupped her mound and groaned into her mouth.

"This is all for me," he growled out. A declaration, not a question.

Because yeah, her slickness was all for him. All because of him. Then he started moving down her body, kissing her slowly, tortuously so, pausing at each breast and taking his sweet time with her nipples until they were rock-hard and wet from his mouth.

Slickness flooded between her thighs as he continued downward.

Sometimes he was incredibly impatient and pounced on her, and others, like now, he slowed right down. He was getting her so damn worked up that she would come if he freaking blew on her clit softly.

"I've missed you," he said as he reached between her legs.

"I can't tell if you're talking to me or my pussy," she said, laughing.

His mouth curved up again as he looked up the length of her body and met her gaze. "Both."

She snickered, but was cut off as he dipped his head lower and flicked his tongue along her slick folds.

Then she forgot about everything but his wicked mouth and speared her fingers through his hair as she rolled her hips against his face. Oh God, he felt so good. So damn good she could barely stand it.

He teased her with his tongue and fingers, sliding two inside her, curling them up so they hit that perfect spot even as he applied pressure to her clit.

"Perfect," she managed to rasp out. It was all she could say as he sucked on her clit, finding that right pressure designed to drive her over the edge.

Something about Daniel always made her crazy like this. He'd taken the time to learn her body, and when he had—he'd played it to perfection.

She clutched onto his head as he continued stroking and teasing her, harder and faster, until a kaleidoscope of colors exploded behind her eyes, her orgasm punching through her like a shock wave designed to turn her to mush.

She'd been remembering just how good things had been between them for two lonely months and now here he was between her legs, making her crazy.

When he looked up the length of her body a long moment later his expression was positively satisfied. And it made her adore him even more. He'd always been so giving, and it made her curse herself for questioning him before. That stupid note had played on every single one of her insecurities, made her think that everything they'd shared was a lie. Looking back, she should have just talked to him about it, expressed her feelings instead of running away like she always did.

Well, she wasn't running now. Nope, she was grabbing onto him with both hands and not letting go.

"On your back," she ordered.

He lifted an eyebrow at her demanding tone but did as she said.

He stretched out on her couch, his big legs taking up all the space, and she realized they weren't going to have enough room. Not even close. "On the floor," she amended, making him grin.

Before he followed her order, he shoved his pants off and lay down on her faux Persian rug.

He looked like a god stretched out before her, all hard muscle and gorgeous thick cock jutting upward just for her. Some of his tattoos moved when he flexed and she found her gaze trailing over all of them. Most were from after his military days—he'd gone crazy covering all his gorgeous skin because he could, because he'd liked the release the temporary pain offered. There was his blue and gold family crest, other symbols of his Scottish heritage, and many more symbolizing his time in the Army. But her attention was captured by one thing right now.

"I've missed you too," she murmured, her gaze on his thick length.

He simply groaned in response, and without warning she took his thick length in her mouth.

"Shit," he rasped out as she sucked him deep.

She grinned around his cock, taking him fully in her mouth again, over and over before she finally lifted her head. "I'm still on birth control," she said quickly. They probably should have talked about this earlier—before they'd gotten turned on and completely naked.

"I haven't been with anyone else," he managed to get out as she teased his balls lightly. She knew exactly what he liked too, exactly how to get him worked up. He hissed in a breath, all those gorgeous muscles in his stomach pulling taut.

"Me neither." So they were good. Better than.

She shimmied up his body, possessed with the need to take him deep inside her. She straddled him, rubbing herself against his hard length. Her inner walls tightened in response as she got ready for him.

"You're killing me," he growled as he grasped her hips.

She thought about teasing him a little longer, but she didn't have the patience or the self-control. Moving slightly, she fully impaled herself on his cock.

He groaned, his hips jerking up to meet hers as she seated herself all the way to the hilt.

She sucked in a breath, closing her eyes as she got used to the feel of him again. Oh yeah, this was the best sensation in the world. Groaning, she let her head fall back, and so very slowly she started to ride him, rolling her hips in a deliberate, sensuous rhythm.

"You're a goddess." His words were harsh and unsteady. And made her inner walls tighten around him even more.

When she looked down at him, his expression was dark and hungry. For her.

Then he took over, flipping her onto her back and pinning her against the rug. He'd always been like that, so desperate for her.

"You can ride me longer the next time," he said through gritted teeth. "I just need this."

She met his mouth with hers, needing to kiss him, needing that extra bond as he started thrusting inside her.

She could feel another orgasm building as he hit her G-spot, and groaned into his mouth at the sensation.

He cupped her breast with one hand and her cheek with the other, the gentle stroking of his thumb against her cheek at odds with the way he was thrusting inside her like a man possessed.

"Gonna come," he rasped against her mouth. "You need another orgasm though," he continued, his words ragged and out of control.

She reached between their bodies and started stroking her clit as he teased her breast.

That was all the stimulation she needed before she went into another free fall of pleasure. This climax was stronger since he was inside her and as soon as she let go, he did too, his thrusts even wilder as he emptied himself inside her.

As he came down from his high, he caged her in against the floor, his forearms on either side of her head as he looked down at her. His breathing was harsh, raspy.

"I think we should put the food away for now."

She grinned up at him. "Yeah?"

"Yeah. We're taking a shower now and you're coming again. We've got two months to make up for."

Her nipples tightened at the thought of coming again, at his roughly spoken words. Since she couldn't find her voice, she simply nodded as he pulled out of her then lifted her into his arms.

Things felt different between them, better. As if all that time apart had solidified that they were meant to be together—that no good came of being apart.

She wasn't walking away from him again.

CHAPTER THIRTEEN

Kathryn twirled once in front of the long mirror, impressed with the transformation. She didn't dress up often but she could admit she felt incredibly feminine, and okay, kind of stunning right now. The body-hugging green dress seemed to have been tailor-made for her. It shimmered when she moved and was the perfect color for her skin tone. And while it was cut lower than she would have chosen, Daniel clearly knew what he was doing—or maybe a personal shopper had picked this out.

Either way, she felt incredible. She'd even begged Chloe to come over and help her with her hair so now she had big, soft curls hanging down her back and framing her face and she looked like a million bucks. She'd had to put Mr. Twinkles up in the guest room because she'd been too afraid that he would jump on her in this dress.

When she realized the time, she texted Daniel. *Everything okay?* He should have been there twenty minutes ago, and for Daniel anything less than twenty minutes early was late. So it was kind of weird that he hadn't contacted her.

She squashed the tension that rose up inside her. It wasn't like he was just not going to show up. After they'd spent Monday night together, they'd spent Tuesday evening in bed as well. Yesterday and today she'd been so busy that they'd only talked on the phone and she desperately missed him. She was pretty sure that Cora knew she was dating Daniel at this point, and probably part of the security team knew it too, but it was what it was. He'd let her keep their relationship quiet for months when they'd been together because of her own fears and he deserved better than that. She was proud that he was hers and wanted him to know that.

When he didn't respond, she tapped her finger against her kitchen countertop. After another ten minutes passed—and then another—real worry settled inside her. They'd planned to meet up early, to share a drink together and then head out. But at this rate the gala would be starting in...half an hour. And it would take twenty minutes to get there from her place. She wasn't supposed to meet him there, right? No, they'd made solid plans. She was just getting all up in her head.

Instead of texting again, she called this time. It rang and rang and rang—finally he picked up.

She'd started to say hey when a sultry female voice said, "Daniel's phone."

She frowned. "Hey, this is Kathryn, is Daniel there?" Maybe it was his assistant and he'd gotten stuck in a meeting.

"He's in the shower, but can I have him call you back?"

She froze for a moment. What the hell? "He's in the shower?"

"Yep," she said, giggling, the sound like shards of glass raking against a chalkboard. "I can go grab him if it's an emergency?"

Ice froze her veins at the woman's words. "Nope. Just have him call me back." With numb fingers, she set her phone on the countertop. Then she pulled out the stool and collapsed onto it, staring off into space and not seeing anything. Was he with another woman right now? No, that didn't make sense. She knew Daniel. This was...this had to be a mistake.

Suddenly her phone dinged. When she saw Daniel's name, a mix of emotions jumped inside her. But as she read through the text, she could feel all the remaining warmth drain from her.

Sorry, I meant to call you earlier but got too caught up at work. Things between us are moving too quickly. You were right to break up with me before. It's not going to work out. I'll keep things professional at the office. But I'll understand if you want to end the contract now.

She stared as hot tears stung her eyes. Was he kidding her? Furiously she texted him back, hating that he'd actually texted her instead of calling. This whole situation was ridiculous. *Are you kidding me? I don't merit a phone call?*

She watched the little bubbles appear and knew he was typing. *I really am sorry, late for the gala and didn't want to deal with hysterics or tears. I know you hate stuff like this so I'm sure it's a relief not to have to go.*

He didn't want to deal with her tears? What the hell? She frowned at the phone, her gut twisting. She had no clue what to say to him at this point. It was like someone else had taken over his body. This wasn't the Daniel she knew.

God, maybe she'd never really known him at all. That was exactly how she'd felt when she'd seen that sticky note in his handwriting. And now…this? She was such a stupid fool. Feeling numb, she left her phone on the countertop, unzipped her dress, let Mr. Twinkles out of the guest room and headed back to her bedroom.

After she'd stripped and washed off all her makeup, the tears finally came. She felt like such a fool for trusting him again. It was as if she'd never known him at all. How could someone be so cruel as to break up by text? She deserved more than that and it broke her heart that this was all he'd given her.

She hadn't been able to get a hold of him today but she'd chalked it up to him just being busy. She'd been busy too, had found a few holes in his new system, but nothing major. Turned out he hadn't been too busy to talk to her, just a coward. He didn't even have the decency to let her know before she'd gotten dressed and done her makeup? Nope, he'd waited until the last minute possible. And was apparently screwing someone else.

And on that thought, another sob built in her throat. She tried to push it down, but there was no controlling emotions like this. More sobs tore free from her as she crawled into bed. Poor Mr. Twinkles jumped up next to her, meowing pitifully as she cried. At least he cared.

CHAPTER FOURTEEN

The next morning, Kathryn felt a little pathetic when she saw she had two missed texts—and secretly hoped one of them was from Daniel telling her that an alien had taken over his body and that he was sorry.

Not that it would matter at this point. He'd broken her trust again, and she was done. Hell, he'd beyond broken her trust. But just because he was a giant dick didn't mean that she wasn't going to go into work and do her job. She'd signed a contract and he could go screw himself.

Using tricks her mom had taught her she actually put on makeup to cover her puffy eyes. It helped a little bit but it didn't make her feel better. She just needed to get through today. Get through one day and then she could drown her pain in ice cream all weekend.

Once she was ready, she made sure she arrived at work early, determined to avoid him at all costs. She didn't think he would terminate her contract or anything, not unless he wanted a lawsuit on his hands, but she wasn't going to give him any excuse at this point. Clearly she'd never known the man at all. Because the Daniel she'd known wouldn't have sent her such cruel texts, wouldn't have ended things like a coward.

By the time she made it to the security floor, where she'd been doing most of her work, she'd managed to give herself exactly eighty billion pep talks. None of them worked.

As she stepped inside the room, Cora and John looked surprised to see her.

"Hey guys," she said, hoping she sounded cheerful. Or at least not like a sad sack. "I'm going to grab some coffee and then dig into some stuff in one of the conference rooms. Just let me know if you need me." She was incredibly thankful that she hadn't planned to work with any of them today, but run some of her own programs instead. At least she wouldn't have to paste on a smile all day while she was crying inside. And next week she'd be off-site so she wouldn't have to risk seeing Daniel at all. Yep, she could totally do this.

They both shared a look and then Cora approached her. She had on one of her dark, tailor-made suits that made her look fierce. Her hair was down today though, in soft waves. "Hey, I'm surprised to see you here."

"Why?" God, did Daniel actually terminate her already or something?

"Look, I know it's absolutely none of my business...but it's okay if you want to leave."

"Why would I want to leave?"

"I mean...you and Daniel."

"There is no me and Daniel." *Not anymore.*

"Oh, yeah. I mean... Look," she lowered her voice, "I saw you guys on the security feed a couple times. I know you got this job because of your skills and reputation," she rushed to add. "I swear I'm not, like, insinuating anything. I get why you want to keep things quiet, trust me.

But I just meant that if you wanted to get out of here, I'm sure Mr. MacArthur would rather you be with him than here."

She blinked. "What are you talking about?"

Her frown deepening, Cora took Kathryn's arm gently and led her to a quiet area at the back of the security room. "He got a really bad case of food poisoning yesterday. He's in the hospital. I thought you knew."

She blinked again. "He got food poisoning yesterday?"

The woman stared at her. "Yeah, I assumed you knew. I mean…I saw you guys kiss on the security camera. I wasn't spying or anything. I just… Maybe I made a wrong assumption. I'm sorry—"

Kathryn's mind reeled. So he hadn't been with someone else? Who the hell had answered his phone and sent her those awful texts? "No, I… What time did he leave?"

"Right after you did, actually. The ambulance showed up maybe ten minutes later. It was a whirlwind here. Everyone was really worried about him."

A strange, sinking sensation settled in her gut. Feeling weird, Kathryn pulled her cell phone out of her purse and brought up the texts from last night. She'd told herself to delete them but now she was glad she hadn't. "So, I'm really sorry for oversharing all this, but I got some texts from Daniel yesterday. Or at least they were from his phone. He broke up with me last night after some woman answered his phone. The texts seemed weird and cruel and so unlike him, but I was so blindsided when I got them. Now… You're sure he got sick right after I left?" Because she'd left early, around three thirty.

Cora frowned. "Yeah, right around four."

She held out her phone so Cora could read the texts. The other woman's expression darkened. "Okay, this is really weird. And I can't imagine Mr. MacArthur using the word 'hysterics.'"

"Me neither." She'd thought it sounded weird last night but now… Something was wrong. It had to be. Oh God, *Daniel.*

"Hold on." Cora pulled out her own cell phone and stepped away to make a call, murmuring quietly into it for a few moments. Then she was back. "I just talked to his assistant and she said she tried to call you but you didn't answer."

"I have no missed calls. Is he okay though? I mean…are you sure it's food poisoning?" Her gut twisted as she tried to wrap her mind around whatever was going on.

Cora stared at Kathryn for a long moment. "I don't like this. Come on," she said. "We're going to the hospital."

That sinking sensation only intensified and Kathryn simply nodded before they hurried out, imagining all sorts of weird scenarios. Nothing made sense though.

Last night she'd thought the texts from Daniel were bizarre and cruel—but she'd been caught up in a wave of emotion. It hadn't even occurred to her that something might be wrong. That would have been like grasping at straws because she didn't want to admit the truth—that he'd ended things with her and broken her heart again. Hell, he'd even referenced her breaking up with him before and it wasn't common knowledge that they'd dated. But if he'd been in the hospital with food poisoning, then he couldn't have texted her.

Nothing about this was right and now fear for his safety ratcheted up inside her.

Thankfully Cora was an expert driver and they made it to the hospital in record time. "I'm just going to drop you off and park," Cora said as she pulled up to the emergency room entrance.

"Thanks. My phone is on me. I'll text you the room number." She knew his parents were out of the country, but she should probably call Sienna or Brodie.

Before she'd even made it to the front desk, she ran into Sienna, who had a small white pastry bag in her hand.

"Kathryn, you're here!" she said, pulling her into a tight hug.

"Yeah, I just found out about Daniel."

"Really?"

"Yeah. At work today, Cora told me." She thought about telling Sienna about the weird texts she'd received but decided not to. It wasn't important right now. Getting to see Daniel and making sure he was okay was all that mattered. If for some crazy reason he actually *had* sent those texts…she'd deal with it later.

"I only found out because I'm friends with a nurse here."

"How bad is it? Cora said he was fine, but..." She couldn't stop the gnawing in the pit of her stomach.

"He's okay. Just needed a lot of hydration. Brodie and I have been waiting for his discharge but the doctor disappeared, so I decided to come grab a snack."

So he really was okay. Kathryn allowed a small bit of relief to slide through her as they headed down a long hallway. "So what happened exactly?"

"He caught some kind of really bad food poisoning. They ended up putting him on an IV to hydrate him. He's fine now. Just exhausted from all the throwing up."

She hated that she wasn't with him now, that she hadn't been with him last night. "I need to call Cora. She came with me." She pulled out her cell phone and went to text the other woman but couldn't get any service. Cursing to herself, she shoved it into her pocket. Cora would just have to get the room number from the front desk.

An elevator ride and a bunch of hallways later, they made it to a small waiting room where a couple families were waiting, as well as Brodie.

Brodie shoved up from his seat when he saw her and pulled her into a tight hug. "Irish, I've missed you!"

She laughed lightly even with the tension coiled in her belly. "I've missed you too."

"Daniel's assistant said you blew her off. I knew she was lying or confused though."

She frowned as she looked between the two of them. None of this was adding up. His assistant had told Cora she hadn't been able to get a hold of Kathryn and now she'd told Brodie that she'd blown her off. She fished out her phone again and held it out. "I never would have blown Daniel off. I got these texts from him last night, but now I'm thinking they weren't from him at all."

Brodie and Sienna read the messages together, then Brodie shoved her phone back at her, his expression all kinds of pissed-off. "I know my brother. He didn't send these. I'll be back."

Before she could respond, Brodie was racing out of the room. *Hell.*

Sienna simply frowned at her. "When we went to see Daniel a few minutes ago, he wasn't in his room. I thought maybe they were in the process of discharging him..." Sienna looked around as if the walls of the room could help her.

Alarm jumped inside her. "None of this feels right." But what the hell could they do?

"No kidding. Because I guarantee Daniel didn't send you those texts. And I was really surprised when his assistant said you blew him off. I knew that wasn't like you, but..." She cleared her throat. "I never really cared for Nicole but I just figured it was a personality clash. She seemed to have a weird fixation on Daniel, almost kind of predatory—but he never noticed so I just chalked it up to me being an overprotective sister."

Before she could respond, Brodie hurried back into the room. "Apparently he's been discharged to his 'fiancée,'" he said, using air quotes. "The description of the woman is exactly like Nicole." Brodie had his cell phone out, his fingers moving quickly across the screen.

What the hell! Tension coiled inside her, pulling into a tight knot. Could his assistant...hurt him? "You guys, what are we going to do? Should we call the..." Kathryn trailed off as Brodie grunted at his phone in triumph.

"What are you doing?" Sienna asked.

"Tracking his damn phone."

"Shit, that's right. We've got that locator app on all of ours."

Kathryn knew what they were talking about because she had a "find a friend" type app on her own phone with her brothers. Carson had insisted, no surprise.

Tension hummed inside her as she waited for Brodie to pull it up. *Come on, come on,* she silently shouted.

"Let's go," he ordered as he hurried back out into the hallway, the two of them hot on his heels.

Chest tight with worry, she kept pace with him. "Where's his phone?"

"It looks like the west side, third level parking lot. Not too far from here."

"That's pretty damn specific."

"Yeah, well, this app isn't available to the public."

Heart in her throat, Kathryn tried to push back the fear bubbling up inside her as they raced down the hallway. She was glad that Brodie seemed to know his way around the hospital because all the hallways looked the exact same to her. But soon they found themselves in front of another set of elevators. They headed down two floors then hurried out and made a quick left.

"This way," he urged as they headed down the rest of the short hallway toward a set of doors that said *EXIT* above them.

The moment he pushed open the double doors into the parking garage, another wave of worry rolled over her. What if...something had already happened to Daniel? No, she refused to think like that.

"You go that way," Brodie snapped at Sienna. "You come with me," he said to Kathryn.

She wanted to argue with him that it would be better if they searched alone to cover more areas, but had to hurry to keep up with him.

Brodie had his phone out and cursed after trying to make a call. "No service in here," he muttered as Sienna peeled off to the left.

Panic punched through Kathryn as they hurried across the parking garage. She wondered if his assistant was actually dangerous or if this was just a bizarre mix-up. This whole situation was just so weird. As they raced to the right, scanning the first aisle of cars, her heart sank. No Daniel.

"There!" Brodie whispered when he spotted Daniel about thirty yards in front of them, slowly making his way down the next aisle of the parking garage.

She started to call out to him but Brodie held up a finger to his mouth.

She wasn't sure why he was silencing her but she nodded as he hurried forward, his movements economic and quick. He tugged her toward the line of cars so they had a bit of cover.

And that was when she saw a four-door sedan backing out of the parking space a few rows in front of Daniel, likely to give him more room to get inside.

Suddenly the car jerked to a halt and the front door swung open.

Before Kathryn could even slow down, Nicole was out of the vehicle and had a gun pointed at the two of them.

Kathryn froze for all of a second before Brodie tackled her, throwing her behind a parked car. Pain exploded in her knees as they hit the pavement, but it all faded as bullets pinged against a nearby car.

"Shit! Nicole, stop!" Daniel shouted.

"Don't you *Nicole* me!"

"What's going on?" Kathryn whispered. She couldn't see Daniel but she could hear the anger in his voice. He was talking so that meant he was alive. Oh God, he had to stay alive.

"You were supposed to be an easy mark! And I'm sick of waiting for you to toss over that bitch," Nicole shouted, her high-pitched voice wavering.

Kathryn and Brodie hurried around to the front of the parked car, crawling forward, trying to stay covered. Damn it, she needed service so she could call the police! At least the parked cars and concrete pillars gave them enough cover.

For now.

Clutching onto her new canister of pepper spray, she held that close. It was the only weapon she had and she would sure as hell use it.

"Come out now or I shoot your boyfriend in the stomach!" Nicole shouted.

Her gut lurched even as Brodie raced forward, weaving in between cars. He was much faster than her, already two cars ahead and so damn close to Daniel. She wasn't sure what he was going to do, but he'd been in the Marines and was now in personal security. He had to have a gun or something…right?

"Now!" Nicole shouted.

Another gunshot rang out and Kathryn flinched, crouching down behind the nearest tire.

Oh God, she couldn't do anything. The woman would kill her if she showed her face and potentially kill Daniel if she didn't. *Think, think, think.* She grabbed a small mirror from her purse and hauled her arm back, throwing it a few cars behind her. Maybe Nicole would think it was her.

Crash! A bullet smashed through the window above her. So maybe her distraction hadn't worked well. She knew if she popped her head up, she was going to get it blown off, but she needed to keep the woman talking. She needed to distract Nicole and let Brodie do whatever it was he was going to do.

"What do you think is going to happen here?" she called out. "You haven't hurt anybody yet," Kathryn added. "You can still walk away from this."

"Shut the hell up. You don't know anything about me, don't know anything about my life," Nicole spat.

"Fine, tell me about your life," she said. Oh God, she hoped there were no innocent civilians nearby. So far she hadn't seen or heard anyone else.

"Don't patronize me!" the woman screamed.

"Nicole, just put the gun down and we can talk," Daniel said quietly.

"Shut up and don't move," Nicole snarled.

Kathryn crouched down under the car and saw Nicole's high-heeled feet moving in her direction.

She inwardly cursed and squeezed in between the front of the 4Runner and the parking pillar. As she peered underneath the car again, she could see Nicole slowly rounding the vehicle—right where Kathryn had been before.

"Stay where you are," Nicole snapped, very likely talking to Daniel. She could see his feet as well, only a few yards away from Nicole.

She had no idea where Brodie or Sienna were, but Brodie had to be nearby, ready to pounce. Her heart was in her throat as she tried to figure out what to do. She needed to get help somehow.

"Over here," she shouted, wanting to get Nicole's attention. Three more shots blasted close by. Bits of concrete fell down on the vehicle next to her, setting the alarm off.

Wincing, she quickly crawled to the next parking spot, hiding on the other side of the car. How many shots could Nicole have left?

Another shot rang out, pinging against the concrete wall four feet above her head and to the left.

Was that six or seven times she'd shot? Trembling, Kathryn got down on her stomach and looked again for Nicole's feet.

Suddenly another car alarm started blaring.

"No!" Nicole screamed and then the gun went off again.

Ping. Ping.

Silence followed, then a thud.

Heart in her throat, Kathryn peered over the top of the car as both Daniel and Nicole rolled on the ground.

Daniel!

She raced around to the back of the car just as Brodie appeared from around the next vehicle, breathing hard and looking as if he'd taken a few punches.

She didn't have time to worry about him as she raced to Daniel and Nicole, her eyes widening at the sight of all the blood on the pavement. "No!"

"Stay back!" Daniel shoved up on wobbly feet, a gun in hand.

That was when Kathryn saw that the blood was pouring from Nicole's shoulder as she writhed in pain against the concrete.

"She had a partner. He's out cold and cuffed," Brodie said as he hurried forward. Ignoring the woman's groans, he flipped her over and secured her wrists behind her with flex cuffs.

Daniel held the gun on Nicole until she was secured. Kathryn threw her arms around Daniel, holding on tight. "Are you sure you're okay?" she demanded, only moving back far enough to get a good look at him. He was exhausted, his face a little hollow and like he needed to eat a few hamburgers. But he was alive!

"I am now. Oh baby, I thought—"

Just then, Sienna and three men in police uniforms stormed the parking garage.

"About time," Brodie muttered, though Kathryn knew that much time hadn't passed. But Daniel could have been killed. Any of them could have.

"She's over here!" Daniel shouted as he shifted to the side, keeping his arm tightly around Kathryn's shoulders.

"And there's another one back there," Brodie added as they approached.

Kathryn had a lot of questions—so many of them—but Daniel was okay. They were all going to be okay.

Emotion swelled inside her, tears pricking her eyes, but she managed to keep them at bay. For now. Soon, she knew she'd break. But she could be strong for a little bit longer. For Daniel.

CHAPTER FIFTEEN

Kathryn leaned into Daniel's hold, snuggling against him on his giant couch. Sienna and Brodie were sitting across from them on another couch and her brother Carson had just stopped by.

It was weird to be back at Daniel's place but she was so glad that all this insanity was behind them. Well, hopefully. It was the reason her brother had stopped by, to update them on everything from hours earlier. They'd all made their statements down at the police station, then headed back here to clean up.

"I can promise that from now on you guys have nothing to worry about. Nicole Granger, aka Nicole Vallow, aka Nicole O'Day, aka who knows how many other pseudonyms she's got, is going to be charged with a lot of crimes. And so will her brother, the man who attacked you at your condo, Kathryn." Carson's jaw tightened once, his rage clear.

Kathryn shuddered as she remembered that man running at her, and leaned closer to Daniel. "I just don't understand what she wanted."

"We don't understand everything at this point either. But apparently she thought you were an obstacle to getting to Daniel. She's milked other men out of millions over the last decade. She seduces them, takes their money, then kills them. Apparently she's very good at what she does. Until Daniel. Her brother's talking fairly freely—she was going to force Daniel to empty his bank account. She decided that working for him and trying to seduce him wasn't going to work—"

"Because he only has eyes for Kathryn," Sienna murmured, smiling softly at Kathryn.

Carson snorted. "Exactly. It sounds like she decided she wasn't walking away from this score no matter what."

"So her brother is going to jail as well? No deals?" Daniel demanded.

"Yes. They'll both do a lot of jail time. They're both wanted in five states. At this point, it might end up turning into a federal case. The team is still figuring out how much shit they have on them."

"I can't believe she got past my security," Daniel said quietly, tightening his grip on Kathryn. "We run extensive background checks."

"My guess is that the background check was fine. Everything you discovered about Nicole Granger was correct—except the fact that she's legally dead. The real Nicole Granger recently died, which is probably why it didn't flag in your system. Or maybe someone dropped the ball, I don't know." Carson lifted a shoulder. "I doubt there's a widespread problem that your company has to worry about."

"I'll look to make sure," Kathryn murmured to him, and he pulled her tighter against him.

"Thank you for stopping by to tell us," Daniel said quietly as he stood.

"Thank you for saving my sister." Carson stepped forward and, surprising Kathryn, pulled Daniel into a quick hug.

Kathryn stood as well and gave her brother a hug. While she loved him and appreciated that he'd come by, she wanted everyone gone. She didn't care that the hospital had checked him out again, she wanted Daniel in bed with his feet up. He did not need to be doing anything right now. Nicole whatever her last name was had poisoned him enough to send him to the hospital and Kathryn wasn't letting him wear himself out.

"I'm going to head out," Brodie said. "Unless you guys need anything?"

Daniel shook his head and hugged his brother too.

"I'll head out with you," Sienna said, but not before she shot Carson a strange look.

Unless Kathryn was mistaken, there was a weird kind of chemistry going on between those two, but she was so not commenting on it or worrying about it now. Nope, the only thing she was worried about was Daniel.

A few minutes later Daniel and Kathryn were finally alone and she collapsed back on the couch with him. For a long moment, she leaned her head on his shoulder and looked at the huge fireplace and mantel. He had pictures of himself and some of his buddies from the army. And there were a couple pictures of the two of them as well. She wondered if he'd just put them back up or if he'd kept them there all along. Either way, it warmed her heart to see them there right now. She could have lost him today.

Anything could have happened and she was still pretty shaken up about it.

She turned to him. "I'm so glad you're okay," she whispered. She'd only said the same words like two million times in the last few hours, but she didn't care because she meant them.

Reaching up, he gently cupped her face and rubbed a thumb over her cheek in a way that made her feel treasured. "I'm glad you're okay too. And we may never know, but I have a feeling she was behind that sticky note you saw on the file. Because I didn't write it."

"Oh hell, you're probably right. She had access to your office and your schedule and knew my comings and goings."

That lunatic had tried to split them up to make her move on Daniel—to steal millions from him. It was all too surreal.

"I love you," they both said at the same time.

She giggled slightly, the band around her chest completely snapping free. With a big smile on her face she leaned into him, wanting to get as close as possible. For the first time in months she felt so damn happy. Even with everything that had happened today, she was with the man she loved.

He tugged her into his lap and right over his thick erection.

Her eyes widened slightly when she felt that bulge. "No way, buddy. You just got out of the hospital and are probably still a little dehydrated. The doctor said—"

"The doctor said I'm fine for physical activity."

"Pretty sure he didn't," she said, even as she shifted against him.

He groaned lightly. "Fine. How about I just lie back and you ride me?"

"I shouldn't…"

He rolled his hips once, his gaze heating. "Come on. We could have died today."

She sucked in a breath as he nipped her bottom lip. "You'll actually let me be in control?"

"Maybe," he growled. "Probably not."

"You are incorrigible."

"True," he said before he covered her mouth with his, no nipping this time but a full claiming.

She fell into that kiss, wrapping her arms around him and just settling into his warmth. She couldn't believe she'd let something come between them, that some awful people had almost ruined what they had. Never again would she doubt this man. He'd never done a thing to make her doubt him. That note had been a lie and her instinct about Daniel had been spot-on. He was one in a million.

And he was the only man she was ever going to love.

When he went for the hem of her shirt, she didn't stop him as he tugged it over her head. And when he undid her bra, she made a move for the hem of his shirt.

She trusted him to tell her if he wasn't up to this. And by the feel of his very hard erection underneath her, he was very much up to this.

Soon she had him naked—wonderfully, gloriously naked—and underneath her. And by the time they'd worked each other up and he slid inside her, his thick length filling her up, she felt as if she'd come home.

There was no other place she wanted to be and no other person she wanted to be with. Ever.

CHAPTER SIXTEEN

One month later

"What's all this?" Kathryn asked as they stepped out onto the roof pool area of Daniel's high-rise building. Lights and balloons were everywhere with little floating flowers in the pool. "It's gorgeous!"

He tightened his fingers against hers. "A little surprise for you."

She looked up at him, surprised that he seemed nervous. Oh God... She racked her brain trying to think if this was some kind of anniversary of theirs. They hadn't been back together long—though according to him those two months didn't count as a breakup. She wasn't good at keeping up with stuff like anniversaries, but she didn't think it was— Oh wait, it was Valentine's Day.

"Oh my God, I forgot to get you a Valentine's Day present." She stared up at him in horror, feeling like the worst girlfriend ever.

He laughed lightly. "That's not for another couple days."

She pushed out a sigh of relief. She'd been so busy working on her current project and of course making love to Daniel every night—and most mornings—that she'd blanked out a few things. Like forgetting to eat breakfast and pay a few bills. This last month had been a whirlwind of work and a lot of sex. Sooooo much sex. Not that she was complaining. Not even a little bit.

As they sat down at a little table that had been set up, he pointed to the edge of the building.

She looked over and all of a sudden fireworks burst across the downtown skyline. "They're beautiful." She absolutely loved fireworks, even though she hated them at the Fourth of July because she always had to combat crowds. So she ended up missing them.

A brilliant kaleidoscope of colors flashed across the night sky—reds, blues, yellows, purples. One after another. "Daniel, I can't believe you did this—" Turning back to him, she stared as he got down on one knee in front of her.

She sucked in a breath as she realized what all this was. He opened up a box to reveal a sparkly diamond ring that she was sure her mother would know the carat and cut of. But all she knew was that it was huge.

"Kathryn Irish, will you marry me?"

For a long moment she couldn't find her voice, but she nodded vigorously. "Yes," she finally rasped out, her throat thick with tears. "Yes, yes!" She didn't even get a chance to let him put the ring on her finger. Instead she threw her arms around his neck, practically tackling him.

Laughing, he scooped her up and sat on the chair, pulling her into his lap as he slid the ring on her finger. The fireworks still exploded in the distance, but they had nothing on the ring he'd just given her. "I thought for sure you knew what I was doing tonight."

Wiping away tears, she shook her head. "I had no idea. Like, not even a little bit. It's so soon," she whispered.

"So what? This is our relationship, we make the rules. And now that you've already been splashed across the stupid society pages, you're going to make an even bigger splash the next time a photographer catches you out in public with this ring."

Groaning, she brushed her lips against his. "You're probably right."

He kissed her back, deepening it for a long moment before he broke away and pointed at the sky again. "I don't want you to miss this."

She laid her head against his shoulder as she watched the fireworks, the brilliant display of colors raining over downtown and the ocean in the distance. She'd never felt more settled, more peaceful, in her entire life.

"I've got champagne on the way up too," he murmured against her hair.

The champagne sounded nice but she didn't care about any of that. She just cared about the man with his arms wrapped tightly around her. The man she'd fallen for so long ago.

He'd given her everything she ever could have wanted. But the most precious thing he'd given her was his heart.

—The End—

ACKNOWLEDGMENTS

This was a fun novella to write and I owe thanks to the usual crowd: Kaylea Cross (always!), Julia for her editing skills, Sarah for beta reading and all the other things she does, Jaycee for another gorgeous cover, my wonderful readers for reading my books. (And talking about them!) You guys are the best!

COMPLETE BOOKLIST

Darkness Series
Darkness Awakened
Taste of Darkness
Beyond the Darkness
Hunted by Darkness
Into the Darkness
Saved by Darkness
Guardian of Darkness
Sentinel of Darkness
A Very Dragon Christmas
Darkness Rising

Deadly Ops Series
Targeted
Bound to Danger
Chasing Danger (novella)
Shattered Duty
Edge of Danger
A Covert Affair

Endgame Trilogy
Bishop's Knight
Bishop's Queen
Bishop's Endgame

MacArthur Family Series
Falling for Irish
Unintended Target
Saving Sienna

Moon Shifter Series
Alpha Instinct
Lover's Instinct
Primal Possession
Mating Instinct
His Untamed Desire
Avenger's Heat
Hunter Reborn
Protective Instinct
Dark Protector
A Mate for Christmas

O'Connor Family Series
Merry Christmas, Baby
Tease Me, Baby
It's Me Again, Baby
Mistletoe Me, Baby

Red Stone Security Series
No One to Trust
Danger Next Door
Fatal Deception
Miami, Mistletoe & Murder
His to Protect
Breaking Her Rules

Continued...

Red Stone Security Series continued...
Protecting His Witness
Sinful Seduction
Under His Protection
Deadly Fallout
Sworn to Protect
Secret Obsession
Love Thy Enemy
Dangerous Protector
Lethal Game

Redemption Harbor Series
Resurrection
Savage Rising
Dangerous Witness
Innocent Target
Hunting Danger
Covert Games
Chasing Vengeance

Sin City Series (the Serafina)
First Surrender
Sensual Surrender
Sweetest Surrender
Dangerous Surrender
Deadly Surrender

Verona Bay
Dark Memento
Deadly Past

Linked books
Retribution
Tempting Danger

Non-series Romantic Suspense
Running From the Past
Dangerous Secrets
Killer Secrets
Deadly Obsession
Danger in Paradise
His Secret Past

Paranormal Romance
Destined Mate
Protector's Mate
A Jaguar's Kiss
Tempting the Jaguar
Enemy Mine
Heart of the Jaguar

ABOUT THE AUTHOR

Katie Reus is the *New York Times* and *USA Today* bestselling author of the Red Stone Security series, the Darkness series and the Redemption Harbor series. She fell in love with romance at a young age thanks to books she pilfered from her mom's stash. Years later she loves reading romance almost as much as she loves writing it.

However, she didn't always know she wanted to be a writer. After changing majors many times, she finally graduated summa cum laude with a degree in psychology. Not long after that she discovered a new love. Writing. She now spends her days writing dark paranormal romance and sexy romantic suspense.

For more information on Katie please visit her website: www.katiereus.com.

Made in the USA
Coppell, TX
19 February 2021